Art Hound
Second Edition

Art Hound
Second Edition

Mike Faricy

Art Hound: Second Edition © Copyright
Mike Faricy 2023

All rights reserved. No part of this publication may be reproduced, stored in a retrieval system, or transmitted, in any form or by any means, electronic, mechanical, photocopying, recording or otherwise, without the prior and express permission of the copyright owner.

This is a work of fiction. All of the characters, organizations, and events portrayed in this novel are either products of the author's imagination or are used fictitiously.

Library of Congress Control Number: 2023915097
paperback ISBN: 978-1-962080-21-7
e-Book ISBN: 978-1-962080-22-4

MJF Publishing books may be purchased for education, Business, or promotional use. For information on bulk purchases, please contact the author directly at mikefaricyauthor@gmail.com

Published by

MJF Publishing
https://www.mikefaricybooks.com

To Teresa
"Would you ever cop on, mister?"

Acknowledgments

I would like to thank the following people for their help and support:
Special thanks to my editors, Kitty, Donna and Rhonda for their hard work, cheerful patience and positive feedback.

I would like to thank Ann and Julie for their creative talent and not slitting their wrists or jumping off the high bridge when dealing with my Neanderthal computer capabilities.

Special thanks to Ann for her patience.

Last, I would like to thank family and friends for their encouragement and unqualified support. Special thanks to Maggie, Jed, Schatz, Pat, Av, Emily and Pat for not rolling their eyes, at least when I was there, and most of all, to my wife Teresa whose belief, support and inspiration has from day one, never waned.

Prologue

I cranked my neck back and forth, and it gave off an audible pop. Then I stretched my arms and legs as best I could in the front passenger seat and pulled my phone out to check the time. Just a little after six in the morning. My car was in the parking lot of the Tryst Hotel and Restaurant two rows behind Farrell Finley's red F150 pickup. Other than stepping out to relieve myself, I'd been sitting in my car since a little after nine last night in the hopes of getting a couple of shots of Farrell and the "girlfriend" he was with.

"Girlfriend" might be too strong a term. She went by the misnomer of Chastity on her escort website, and he'd paid for the privilege of her company two or three times before, at least, that was how many times I was aware of. Foolishly, he'd made those arrangements on a home computer.

I guess he didn't lie about being out of town for the night. The Tryst Hotel was a good six miles over the state line and into Wisconsin, making it about twenty-four miles from his front door in Saint Paul. I knew Farrell had to be at his desk at nine, and he had to drop Chastity off someplace back in town, so I figured I'd be able to get my pictures in the next hour or so.

The parking lot was slowly filling up with the early morning breakfast crowd. It looked like mostly regulars since it was off the interstate by a good mile, and the average age of the folks pulling in appeared to be north of sixty. At five minutes after seven, Farrell and Chastity walked out of the hotel.

Bleach-blonde Chastity looked the part in a skimpy top, exposing a midriff and love handles. She wore blue-jean cutoffs that looked like they were spray-painted on and didn't quite cover. She carried her luggage, what appeared to be a small black velvet bag probably filled with battery-operated appliances, slung over her shoulder. They were holding hands and laughing as they headed toward Farrell's pickup truck.

He was a relatively large guy with close-cropped reddish-blonde hair. He was light-skinned, as opposed to pale, with freckles, lots of freckles. I guessed he'd let himself go over the last ten plus years, and the once narrow waist now hung over his belt. That said, he was still the kind of guy you wouldn't want to push, and I certainly didn't want to this morning.

I started taking pictures using a digital camera. The time and date would appear in the lower right-hand corner of each image. They suddenly took a different route than I had expected, veering over a couple of parking places so Farrell could appraise a classic Trans Am parked in the lot. The problem with their new route was the sign touting the Tryst Hotel wouldn't show up in my pictures.

I made a command decision and quietly slipped out of my car. I slinked over about a half-dozen parking spaces to the right until I had them aligned with the hotel sign.

Click. Click. Click.

"Good God, I think this here is a sixty-nine, part of Pontiac's limited edition release. What a beauty. But I don't know if I'd be letting it sit out here in a parking lot overnight."

Click. Click. Click.

"Some idiot's liable to scratch it or open a door and hit the damn paint job."

"Hey, you know that jerky guy over there?" Chastity asked.

Click. Click

"What?"

"That weirdo over there, see him kinda hiding behind the green car. He's been taking pictures of us. Hey, creep, how 'bout this?" Chastity said, then lifted her skimpy top, exposing herself, struck a pose, and gave me the finger.

Click.

"Just what in the hell do you think you're doing, Jackass?"

Click.

Oh, oh.

Farrell started heading toward me. He wasn't huge, but he was bigger than me, and right now he didn't look happy. I started to casually walk toward my car, a 2007 Dodge Caliber. After about four paces, I figured it might make sense to just get in the car and flee the scene so I started running, as fast as I could. So did Farrell. Unfortunately, Farrell had been a high school football star, and I hadn't.

"Get him, Farrell, get him, woo-hoo, go, baby, go," Chastity screamed as she jumped up and down.

We met at the driver's door of my car.

"Who the hell are you?" Farrell shouted then punched me in the face.

"Back off, Farrell, I'm just doing my job." My head suddenly bounced off the side of the car, and I saw stars for a moment. I took a couple of quick steps back. Farrell clenched both fists, got an even meaner look on his face, and took a step toward me. I flung the car door open and caught him right between the eyes. He landed on the ground in a sitting position, looking stunned. I reached into the car, pulled the pistol out from underneath the driver's seat then calmly closed the car door.

"Hey, Farrell. No offense, but you're a real asshole. You got a wife and three kids at home, and your wife is wise to you. If I were you, I'd get my ass back to town and try and figure out how you're going to fix things if it isn't too late already."

"You can't tell me what to do."

"Hey, you listening? I just did. Now get the hell out of here before I change my mind."

He slowly got to his feet and shook his head as if to clear it. His lips were split, already swelling, he had a trail of blood dripping out of his right nostril and a large angular bruise in the middle of his forehead. "You better watch out, 'cause I'm gonna find out who the hell you are."

"You got bigger problems than me right now, Farrell. Just get in your truck and go home."

He seemed to think about that for a moment, looked at the pistol I was holding, then backed up a few paces before he turned and quickly headed for his truck. He climbed in, slammed the door, then fired up his F-150 and screeched out of the parking lot, leaving a cloud of exhaust and bleach-blonde Chastity in the dust.

"Farrell, hey Farrell, baby, wait. Wait for me, baby, wait," Chastity called. She ran after him for a car length or two, then stopped and screamed, "You worthless bastard, I'm glad you didn't get any."

Farrell's pickup raced down the road and faded into the distance.

I slipped behind the wheel of my car and headed in the same direction Farrell had just gone, but nowhere near as fast. I watched Chastity in the rearview mirror as she headed back into the Tryst Hotel.

One

Later that day, just across town . . .

"Are you f'ing kidding me? You painted that on my dining room wall?" Colleen asked.

Demarcus Cantrell stood back and admired his work, a naked woman eating an apple lying on what appeared to be a massive dinner platter. He'd even incorporated her mother's china pattern into the platter. He decided some attention was still required, the shadowed area beneath the right breast, and perhaps just the slightest bit of warmth added to the lips, but otherwise, yet another work of artistic genius.

"The room just needed something. I can't always be restricted to a small canvas, my precious. Just think of the value it will add to the house."

"Value added to the house? My house? That's it, Demarcus, I've had it. I want you out of here, right now."

"Precious, relax, calm down. We've both had a long workday. Now what do you say you make me some fresh coffee and both of us lunch while I clean up?"

"Did you hear me? I said, get the hell out of my house. Now," she screamed, then grabbed an easel and a canvas from the corner and marched toward the door.

"Precious, now calm down."

"My name is Colleen. You call me 'Precious' again, and I'm going to stab you. I'm coming off a double shift, and you've spent the last sixteen hours painting a naked woman on my dining room wall." She tore the front door open and tossed the easel into the yard, then flipped the canvas out on top of it. "Get moving, mister. I have had it. I've paid the freight around here for over four months, and this is what I come home to? You are so done."

"I think we should talk. You don't seem to understand."

She ran into the kitchen, and a moment later, he heard a drawer being pulled open. She was back in the dining room, eyes flaring and baring her teeth. She held a very large, very sharp butcher knife.

"Whoa now, Precious, err, umm, Colleen, calm down. Maybe you'd like it better if she was blonde. I can change that."

"Ahhh," she screamed, red-faced as she slashed at him with the knife.

"Calm down, my, I mean, Colleen. Just calm down."

"Killing you would be so simple right now and probably the only way to bring any value to your wretched, worthless paintings. Now, I'm going upstairs to the guest room for some much-needed sleep. I'm taking this knife with me. When I wake up, if you and all your paintings are still here, I'm really going to kill you."

"Darling, I think you may be overreacting."

"Please don't think. It drives me crazy when you try and think. Please. Do. Not. Think," she screamed.

"Okay, okay," he said, pulling a chair between them for added protection.

"I'm going to close my eyes. I've worked a double shift, and right now, I have a very, very short fuse. For your own good, do not be here when I wake up. Goodbye, Demarcus. It's been a real education," she said, then turned and headed up to the bedroom.

He examined his work for a moment, decided it would only take a moment or two to warm the smile and attend to the shadow before he packed his belongings, and so set to work. An hour later, he stepped back from the wall and viewed his creation with an air of satisfaction. Yeah, he was definitely on to something here. He decided to take a couple of photos and upload them into a file. If Colleen didn't wish to participate, well, that would be her loss. He thought for a moment and wondered where he could go.

Two

Heidi raised her eyebrows and said, "Oh, come on, Dev, a poetry reading, it'll be fun. God only knows you could use the culture, plus there just might be something in it for you afterward." I immediately got on board.

Finally, it was Friday night after what had been a couple of grueling weeks for both of us. Heidi was dealing with some initial public offering she'd promoted to investors that was finally beginning to perform after two weeks of heated phone calls from people with too much money and way too much time.

Me? Let's see. I got dumped by a woman named Margo before the relationship even got off the ground. I thought things were starting to look up when she left me the polite phone message at four in the morning that said, 'Things aren't working out,' followed by another message two minutes later where she just screamed, 'Fuck you,' and hung up.

I drove over to her house that night with Morton, my golden retriever, serving as a witness, hoping to calm Margo down. That thought quickly went from bad to really bad when she began screaming and frightened Morton, who ended up leaving a puddle on her kitchen floor. The two of us were out the door about ninety seconds after that. My only thought was if I heard the screen door open behind me as I walked to my car it was everyone for themselves because I was going to run.

Anyway, that was the highlight of my social life. Business-wise, the good news was I got the somewhat compromising photos of Farrell engaged in a stupid extramarital affair. The bad news was he was a one-time high school football star and caught up with me.

"How does that eye feel?" Heidi asked. "It still looks pretty sore."

"The swelling has gone down. I can touch it now, and it doesn't hurt, too much. The blurry vision has pretty much disappeared." I was driving us in Heidi's car to the poetry reading. Some high school friend of hers who had published her fifth or sixth book of poems. I'd never even heard of the woman, let alone the poetry books, but then again, I'm pretty much out of the demographic, well, unless the poem happens to rhyme with Nantucket.

"I think that's the place up there on the corner," Heidi said. She half pointed to a two-story stucco building on the corner. Illegible graffiti in black spray paint ran along the side of the building. One of the front windows was covered with a sheet of plywood hosting more spray-painted graffiti, this time in red.

"That dive on the corner?"

"Yeah, I guess. I mean, it looks kind of dumpy," Heidi said.

"Then it fits right into the neighborhood, that church we just passed a block back had a 'No Loitering' sign out in front." I pulled alongside the curb and parked behind a shiny black Mercedes, probably the neighborhood pimp's car.

"We better hurry, I don't want to miss anything," Heidi said and jumped out of the car. I checked the backseat to make sure nothing was left in the car because it wouldn't be there when we returned, and we'd no doubt have a window to replace. "Are you coming?" she called from the sidewalk.

We hurried inside, not that we needed to. With our attendance, the crowd, including poet, author, and reader, Eunice, increased to nine people. Her first poem, I can't recall the title, went on for twenty-three minutes, and didn't rhyme. When she was finished, everyone gave polite applause except for me, only because I'd drifted off to sleep. Heidi elbowed me as she clapped. "That was wonderful," she said and glared at me.

I got the message and fought to remain awake for the next hour and a half through a few more monotone readings. Finally, Eunice slid off her stool and took a deep bow. I clapped, but only because she was finally finished. Heidi purchased her book and had Eunice sign it. Then we stepped over to the hors d'oeuvres table, actually a card table with an open bottle of Jameson and a stack of plastic cups. I poured myself an hors d'oeuvre.

"You're the only one drinking," Heidi said under her breath as she smiled at a well-dressed older couple walking past. The guy made his way to the card table and poured himself a glass.

"I'm the only one who's recovered. Everyone else is still numb from the neck up."

"Mrs. Martin," Heidi said as the older woman approached. "I'm Heidi."

"Yes, yes, of course, Heidi. It's been so long. How wonderful to see you. And thank you so much for supporting Eunice."

"My pleasure. Very interesting."

"Mmm-mmm," the woman said and then looked in my direction. "And is this, your husband?"

"A friend of mine, Dev Haskell. He's been interested in Eunice's work. Dev, this is Eunice's mom. She always took such good care of us when we were absolutely awful teenage girls."

"Oh, nothing of the sort, now stop," the woman laughed and extended her hand. "How nice to meet you, Mr. Hassle."

I shook her hand just as the guy I guessed was her husband joined us with his drink.

"Dev, this is Eunice's father," Heidi said.

He raised his glass in my direction but didn't say anything. The ladies had two minutes of worthless conversation, and then Eunice's father downed his Jameson, and they departed.

"You want to say something to Eunice?" I said and finished the last of my drink.

"No, she doesn't like to be hassled by fans."

"What? Hassled?"

"If you're finished, we should just go."

"Did I miss something?"

"Dev?"

Three

Heidi wedged two pillows behind her and sat up in bed. My Golden Retriever, Morton, had snuck up onto the bed and taken over the spot where I'd slept. I handed her a cup of coffee, and she took a sip. "Mmm-mmm, thanks. What's that I smell?"

"I'm cooking you breakfast."

"Pancakes?"

"Yeah, blueberry pancakes, with real maple syrup and some smoked bacon. You just sip your coffee and take your time. I'll call you when it's ready, maybe fifteen minutes or so."

"Oh, you're so sweet, Dev."

"Well, sorry if I didn't catch on to the cultural stuff last night. I just—"

"Oh, God, I'm sorry I dragged you to that. Wasn't it awful?"

"Awful? I thought you liked it?"

"Liked it? Are you kidding? Oh my God, it was just dreadful. They always are."

"Well then, why did we even go?"

"I always try to support Eunice. We've been friends since junior high."

"But you don't seem to have anything in common with her. You didn't even talk to her."

"I know, I know. We were really close, once, and then she took a strange turn, she started hanging with the wrong crowd, got into drugs. After high school, we went in totally opposite directions. She's recovered now, at least I think she is, but the damage is there. Oh, she used to be so talented and fun and—"

"And no offense, but she's a real downer. Those poems, they didn't even rhyme. And then she doesn't want people talking to her at the end? Really strange."

"Yeah, including her parents. She doesn't want to talk to them. It upsets her. Maybe it reminds her of what could have been if she wasn't such a mess, but that's not nice. I don't mean it like that. I know, I know. I keep going to these things hoping someday I'll walk in and there my old girlfriend will be, smiling and joking. I don't know. It's just so sad. I don't know what it would take to get her back if it can even be done."

"What do her folks think?"

"God bless them, they've had years of heartache. She was bright, intelligent, fun, interesting, and then, eventually, a burnout. Their only child and, well, you saw."

"Grim. I better get back to breakfast. Take your time. Morton, you bum, come on, you can go outside."

"Oh, he can stay."

"No way. Just close the bedroom door when you come down so he doesn't eat your thong again. Come on, Morton, let's go."

Morton took his time, hopping off the bed. He stretched on the floor for a long moment, giving me a look to see if I'd head downstairs so he could hop back up next to Heidi.

"Come on, Morton, get going," I said, and he grudgingly followed. He lingered near the front door for a long moment and gave a loud bark.

"No, come on, out the back, let's go." I had to call him once again from the kitchen before he finally followed. I figured he was angling for a walk, but he seemed to change his mind once he stepped into the kitchen and realized there was bacon on the stove.

"Outside first, then we'll see about breakfast." He hurried outside and was back at the door after just a minute or two.

I called Heidi down for breakfast. She walked into the kitchen wearing my black Ramones t-shirt. Thankfully, just short enough not to cover. "You closed the bedroom door?"

"Mmm-hmm. This looks great," she said, as I slid a plate of blueberry pancakes and smoked bacon across the counter to her, then filled up her coffee mug. "Bon Appétit."

"Oh, God, French. Who knew?"

"It's all that culture I absorbed last night."

"Yeah, right."

We talked for a long time over breakfast. She grabbed a shower while I cleaned up in the kitchen, then came down all dressed just as I finished up.

"You want another coffee? Don't feel like you have to go."

"I've got a couple hours of office work I have to get done."

"It's Saturday, take a break."

"Wish I could, but I need to get this wrapped up before Monday. I've investors coming in at nine."

"You sure?"

"Yeah, but I'll take a rain check."

"You got it," I said. "Come on. I'll walk you to the door."

"Oh, ever the gentleman," she laughed. She gave me a quick kiss at the door, then patted Morton on the head as I opened the door.

"Ufff, ouch, God," the man grunted as he fell into the front entry, and his head bounced off the floor.

Heidi shrieked.

Morton barked and ran behind Heidi.

I just shouted, "Demarcus? What the hell are you doing here?"

Four

We'd been hauling easels, tubes of oil paints, canvases…a lot of canvas, a toaster, a half-dozen ceramic angelfish to hang on the wall, a stained glass lamp with a brass naked lady base and just an awful lot of junk into the living room for the past half-hour while Demarcus told me the story, at least his version of the story. Just now, I was carrying four more canvas paintings and leaning them against the dozen or so of the same size I'd already stacked against the wall.

Demarcus had hold of a faux-leather, high-backed office chair patched in three different places with fluorescent green duct tape. He rolled it in the door behind me then pushed it across the entry with his foot, where it bounced against the wall.

"I don't know, man, it's like I said, she just all of a sudden went off the deep end and was threatening to kill me. The next thing I know, she's heading up to the guest room with a butcher knife, telling me I have to be gone when she wakes up. Based on the circumstances, I decided it maybe wasn't the best time to try and reason with her."

"Maybe she was just, you know, exhausted from doing that double shift."

"Yeah, maybe, but I've been sensing something like this for quite some time. She's mentioned me getting a job, seems like every other day for the past month. Christ, can't she tell I'm an artist? I had canvases stored in every room on the first floor. I don't know," he said, then shook his head, suggesting none of it made any sense.

"You guys got financial trouble? I don't need to know specifics, but that can add a lot of stress to any situation."

"Well, it would certainly help if I could sell some of my artwork. But she knew that was going to be difficult when I suggested I move in with her. I mean, it seemed like a good idea at the time. After all, she's really hot. Hell, now I'm thinking she just wanted some idiot to shovel the sidewalk or cut the damn grass. You know?"

"You cut the grass and shoveled her sidewalk?"

"No. God, are you kidding? First of all, when I feel the need for artistic expression, I have to pay attention, that comes first and foremost. I'm a professional, after all. Then the other thing is, if I throw my back out using a snow shovel or pushing the damn lawnmower, that's sure not going to do much for my artistic career, now is it?"

"Yeah, but you know, maybe if you did a couple of those things around the place, it might maybe calm her down. It's hard keeping a house up. She's working, pulling double shifts, there's always going to be something that needs to be fixed or replaced in any house."

"Come on, and she's always worried about keeping her figure. She goes to the 'Y' almost every day. I thought I was helping out by having her do some physical labor around the place. It's free. She doesn't even have to pay a membership fee or anything. But, oh no, that won't do. She'd much rather read me the riot act, ruin the mood. I don't know, I can't figure her out."

I more or less missed that last part since I was outside bringing in two suitcases and a very heavy duffel bag. One of the suitcases was dark blue with creamy-colored or maybe just yellowed leather along the sides and looked to be about sixty years old. The other was black and looked somewhat better, although it was missing a set of wheels, which meant I had to pick it up instead of rolling the thing. The large duffel bag, absolutely crammed with clothes, was strapped over my shoulder. The strap felt like it was cutting into the side of my neck.

"Oh, yeah, you could probably drag that duffel bag back by your washing machine. I need to do some of that laundry. Feel free to throw a load in while you're back there."

"No, thanks. Hey, thought you were painting bowls of fruit, when did you start doing that stuff?" I nodded toward the stack of canvases leaning against the wall. All of them looked like they'd been used as a drop cloth. Just splatters of different colored paint, it looked like maybe three colors to a canvas, red, white and black, or orange, yellow and green. Two of them had maybe five colors splattered across them. Rolls of canvas, apparently all yellowed with age or else they'd been out in the sun too long, were now standing in two corners of my living room.

"Well, I did these for a year or two. I guess maybe a little too advanced for this town."

"A year or two? How many did you do?"

"How many? Those twelve there, I was on a roll, cranking out one a month, really pushing it."

"One a month?"

"Yeah, like I said, I've been really pushing it."

"You sold any?"

"That's not the real point. And, before you say anything, Colleen bitched about that, too, so whatever it is, I've already heard what you were about to say. Dev, I don't expect you to get this, but I'm constantly pushing the frontiers, and first of all, you have to be in the mood, really in the mood, to create these. Here, check this one out," he said, picking up a canvas from the stack. It was a black background, with drips and splashes of red, white, and purple. "What does it say to you?"

I wanted to say something along the lines of 'bullshit.' I figured I could do one of those things in about five minutes with my eyes closed. "Man's inhumanity to man?"

"Good, very good. Wow, I'm surprised. Actually, it represents the juxtaposition of mother earth to life, at least as we know it. Get it? Dark space and the very beginnings of life forms from which we've all descended. You go back far enough, we're all related."

I shook my head and wondered who in the hell would buy something like that, let alone hang it up somewhere. "You sell any of those?"

"I just got done saying, it's not about selling them. My talent has nothing to do with the monetary factor."

"So, then, why were you doing it?" Right now, I was thinking if I had been Colleen, I would have done this a long time ago. No, check that, I would never have gotten involved with Demarcus.

"Why was I doing it? Dev, it has to be done."

"But, then, when did you start doing the nude thing, like on Colleen's dining room wall?"

"That's been a recent occurrence. If you're interested, I'll email you an image."

"Yeah, I'd like to see it."

"Anyway, that's not important. This is the future," he said, then carefully set the splattered canvas back in the stack.

I looked around the place. My living room was crammed full of junk, all of which belonged to Demarcus. "So, ahh, how long are you planning to stay?"

"Shouldn't be more than a day or two, just until I get a couple of different options worked out. Say, you want to grab those suitcases and take them up to your guest room? I'm gonna grab a beer and make a sandwich. You want anything?"

Five

It was just past noon on Monday when she called. Morton and I had already been in the office for a few hours and I was taking a lunch break across the street at The Spot. "How's it going," Heidi asked.

"Just fine if boring is your thing. I'm plowing through a stack of job applications for an insurance company trying to find any discrepancies."

"Are you finding any?"

"No, but about all I can get people to do when I call is confirm the applicants worked for them. No one is going to tell me if the person was fired, or stole things or was a lousy employee. Seems like the most I can get is a confirmation of dates of employment, nothing more."

"Sounds dreadful," Heidi said, then groaned for emphasis.

"That about sums it up. What's up with you?"

"Usual. The real reason I'm calling is to see what happened with that Demarcus guy who apparently slept on your front porch. Where did you send him?"

"Send him? God, up to the guest room."

"The guest room? At your place?"

"Yeah. Look, I know what you're going to say. But it's just for a little while, maybe a day or two," I said and tried to sound hopeful.

"No offense, but hasn't he already been there for two days? I know you're trying to help, but that's more than a little crazy. He's liable to drive you nuts."

"There's no liable about it, he's already doing that. After a weekend with him at my place, I was actually anxious to get to the office this morning. He was working on some painting of Colleen until about sunrise, then drew up a list of grocery items I need to get. Apparently, I'm out of Jameson, among other things."

"You?"

"Yeah. Well, I checked, there was about a half-inch left in the bottle. I guess he needed fuel for his artistic soul or something."

"The sooner you get him to leave, the easier it's going to be. Maybe, you could tell him you have house guests coming."

"Not a bad idea, but I'm not sure that would register. I think he'd just figure he'd have to share the bed. He's way out there. Don't get me wrong. If I had a problem, he'd do anything, maybe, I think, if you asked him, but lending a helping hand doesn't seem to be his strong suit."

"Oh, Dev, the sooner, the better. If for no other reason than your own sanity."

"I know, I know."

"You interested in dinner tonight?"

"I could be talked into that. You want to meet me somewhere?" I asked and held my breath. Fine if we met somewhere, but dinner *at* Heidi's always meant she had a plan for working off the meal later that night.

"I was thinking I'd pick up a couple of steaks, and you could do them on my grill."

Right answer. "I'll pick up some wine if that works."

"Perfect. See you around seven. You can relax and tell me the latest horror story, but the sooner, the better as far as having him leave, Dev."

"See you at seven, and thanks, Heidi." She disconnected, and I thought for a long moment. She was right, of course, the sooner I got rid of Demarcus, the better it would be, for both of us. I began to plot what I was going to say.

Six

On the way home, we stopped at the grocery store and worked off the list Demarcus left for me. Eighty-seven dollars later, Morton and I were headed for the liquor store to replenish my supply of Jameson.

I had five bags of groceries, not to mention the 4.5-liter bottle of Jameson. I carried everything up to the front porch in three trips then unlocked the front door. Demarcus's ratty office chair and four boxes of junk that belonged to him were still stacked up against the far wall. Demarcus had taken the five or six boxes he'd set on the couch and placed them on the living room floor so he could stretch out on the couch and take a nap, which was where he was when I opened the door. I stood there staring, expecting him to wake up, but it didn't happen.

"I'm home," I called. He wrinkled his nose a couple of times, but other than that gave no real indication he'd heard me. "Hey, Demarcus, wake up, sunshine. I got groceries to carry in," I said, then waited until he slowly started to open his eyes in response.

I took the two bags I was carrying, headed for the kitchen, and started to put things away. Once I had everything put away, I walked back out to the front entry. Demarcus was snoring again.

"Hey, dip shit, let's go. Grab some groceries here and bring them back to the kitchen."

"Huh, what? Oh, you're home? Mmm-mmm, give me just a minute."

I hauled the next two bags into the kitchen and put things away. Still no Demarcus, so I walked back out to the front entry. At least he was off the couch. I just couldn't tell where he was hiding. I heard the toilet flush upstairs a moment later, shook my head, grabbed the last grocery bag along with the 4.5-liter of Jameson from the car, and headed back to the kitchen.

By the time Demarcus wandered into the kitchen, everything was put away, including the Jameson, which I'd hidden under the kitchen sink. I was folding up the grocery bags and stuffing them into recycling.

"Anything I can help with?"

"Already done. Hey, how'd it go finding a little more permanent place to land? It's got to be a pain living out of a suitcase."

"Mmm-mmm, yeah, I suppose I should get going on that, you know looking for a place. You got any ideas?"

"Maybe try Craigslist. There's a couple of buildings over on Portland Ave with signs in front. I don't know what the rent would be, maybe give them a call. You could Google available sites online, and you'll probably get a bunch of options. You'll wanna get going on that. I got a couple of old Army pals coming in later this week. They're bringing their wives, and their kids, so it's going to get pretty crowded," I said, hoping my lie was convincing.

"That mean I'll have to move into your room?" he said. He sounded like it might be an inconvenience for him.

"No. It means I need you and all your stuff out of here by Wednesday at the latest. I'm having cleaners in Thursday to get the place ready," I lied.

"Well, here's the problem, or at least part of the problem. I still have a ton of stuff sitting over at Colleen's, because I ran out of time, you know, fearing for my life and all. I'll need to get that stuff out of there, but I probably shouldn't be the one to go over and get it, just from a safety standpoint."

"Maybe call her and see if you can't work something out."

"Yeah, I suppose I could do that. God, I hate to bug her, she can get so bitchy, so damn fast."

I was beginning to see things from Colleen's side, and four or five months of putting up with this guy did not sound like getting bitchy very fast to me.

"Maybe try and contact her online. You could email her or send her a Facebook message or something."

"Yeah, I suppose I could do that, maybe."

"Or you could just pick up the phone and call her."

"Mmm-mmm. Hey, what are we doing for dinner?"

"*We* aren't doing anything. You can cook your own dinner, and I'm out on a hot date."

"Three's company, but four's a crowd," he said and looked hopeful.

"No, that's two's company and three's a crowd. This is going to be a private endeavor, very private, just me and Hei…this lady I met," I said, not wanting him to know any more about my evening than the fact I wouldn't be around to cook him dinner. "I'm going to hit the shower, get ready, and then head out of here. There's hamburger in the fridge, pasta in the pantry, help yourself, and clean up any mess. Don't forget to contact Colleen and get the rest of your stuff out of her place. Although it might make sense to move it from her place to wherever you land, no point in handling it twice if you don't have to."

He nodded, suggesting that sounded like a good idea.

I went upstairs to take a shower. My shaving cream was still on the vanity, along with my razor. I never leave them out. Apparently, Demarcus had forgotten his. The hot water hadn't been completely turned off, and so a small but steady stream had been running in the bathroom sink for probably the last eight hours. I put my finger under the faucet. The water was cold.

There were three towels hanging on the racks when I left this morning. All three were now lying on the floor, soaking wet and crumpled. I turned off the water in the sink, tossed the wet towels down the clothes chute then pulled two more towels out of the linen closet. I turned on the shower, hoping against hope, surprise, surprise, there was no hot water. But then, why would there be?

"That was fast," Demarcus said. He was seated at the kitchen counter, drinking one of my beers. The faucet was running in the sink. Not into a pan or anything to catch the water, it was just running down the drain.

"What the hell are you doing with the water?" I said and turned it off.

"Hey, don't, man. I'm waiting for it to get hot so I can cook some pasta."

"Then just fill a pan and turn the stove on to get it to boil."

"Oh, yeah, I s'pose that'd work. Probably want to get it checked out, all the same, your hot water sure as hell isn't working all that great."

"Probably because you left it running upstairs in the bathroom and, over the course of an entire damn day, you managed to empty the hot water heater."

"You sure?"

"Very. I turned it off up there. Looks like when you shaved, with my razor I might add, you left it running. By the way, sorry to sound like your mom, but one towel is all you get for your stay. Christ, you left three of them soaking wet and lying on the floor. What did you do? Take them in the shower with you?"

"Oh, ahhh, not exactly. See, I wanted to take a bath and just lounge in the tub for a while, so I filled the tub…I guess it kind of overflowed or something."

"Kind of overflowed?"

"Yeah, a lot of water on the floor. That's why the towels were there. I mean, I soaked it up. The rest just kind of disappeared."

Oh Christ, I thought and hurried into the den. A ten-foot area all around the antique fixture in the center of the ceiling had turned a dark grey, wet plaster from water leaking through the bathroom floor just above it. I wanted to kill. But instead, I headed back into the kitchen.

"Hey, man, grab me another beer, will you?" Demarcus said, then finished the one he'd been drinking. I noticed it wasn't his first.

"No."

"What?"

"I said no, I'm not getting you another beer. In fact, here's the deal, Demarcus. I love you, but in little more than a weekend, you've become a major pain in the ass. I can't shower because you drained the hot water. I've got a ceiling in my den that's liable to collapse because you let the bathtub overflow. You've got your shit scattered all over my first floor, and you drank most, if not all, of my Jameson. Now, you told me you would be here for just a day or two. I'm a generous guy, so I'm going to go the extra mile and give you a little extra time. You need to be out of here the day after tomorrow. And you need to call Colleen and get your shit out of her place, too. I don't want you bringing it here, so figure something out. Okay?"

"God, sorry, man, if my bad luck pissed you off."

"Demarcus, don't be sorry. I just need you out of here the day after tomorrow. Can we agree on that?"

"Yeah, I suppose, I mean in the end, it's your place, and I appreciate you being so generous and all. Didn't mean to let the water run all day, or overflow the bathtub or drink all the Jameson. Sorry, dude."

"Don't worry about it. Look, day after tomorrow, I'll even help you move, okay? We'll get the rest of your stuff out of Colleen's. Right now, your top priority is to find a place you're going to go, got it?"

He nodded. I opened the refrigerator and reached into the twelve-pack to get a beer for him. There were only three left, and the pack had been unopened as of this morning. I made note of the fact, opened the beer and handed it to him, which seemed to brighten his face, at least just a little.

"You're off to that Katie's house?" he said.

"No, Heidi's," I answered, then could have kicked myself for mentioning her name.

"Oh yeah, that hot looking woman from the other morning. Well enjoy. I guess I'll just hang here and try and keep myself busy."

"Maybe, if you could find time in your busy schedule, you could check out a place to move to. You know, rather than waiting until the last minute and then having to maybe settle for second best."

Seven

Heidi was curled up on her couch in the living room, wearing a very small black negligee. "So he isn't actually gone yet?" she said. For a change, her hair was a natural color, well except for the pink highlights on top. The lights were so dim they were almost off, the gas fireplace was set on low. She had Pandora dialed up on her computer, and nice music was softly playing in the background. She was sipping a glass of red wine. I was drinking a beer. Our steak dinner had been nothing short of wonderful, and I finally had Demarcus pretty much out of my mind.

"He's still there, but just for another day or so, then he's gone. I took your advice and told him I have guests coming, and he was going to have to leave."

"He bought that excuse."

"I didn't leave him any other option. Look, I'm nice and relaxed, we had a wonderful dinner, you look absolutely fab, so let's change the subject to something more interesting. You want another glass of wine?"

"Maybe just half a glass. I want to remember the later-on part of the night," she said and set her glass on the coffee table.

Ever since I've known her, Heidi has been on a lunar calendar. Her hormones really start flowing when the moon is full. I teased her about it once, and she suggested that if I wanted to continue to partake in the experience, it might be wise if I just changed the subject. I'd checked before coming over, and tonight was a full moon. That explained the invite, the steaks, the negligee, everything, not that I was complaining.

I began to top off her glass.

"Whoa, whoa, that's enough. Like I said, I want to remember."

"Oh, yeah, sorry. Let me ask you something." My cellphone suddenly rang. I glanced at the clock on the mantel, damn near eleven.

"Who calls at this hour?" Heidi said, not sounding happy.

I pulled my phone out but didn't recognize the number.

"Hello?"

"Dev, oh great, I wasn't sure this was your number."

"Demarcus?" I said and looked over at Heidi. She rolled her eyes and set her glass back down.

"Yeah. My cell disappeared, can't find it anywhere, so I went out and grabbed this pay as you go."

"Well, you got my number. Look, I'm a little involved right now. I'll catch you in the morning."

"Oh, yeah, sorry to interrupt, man. Umm, good luck."

"Thanks, bye," I said and hung up.

"What was that about?"

"You don't want to know. He lost his phone."

My cell rang again. "Demarcus," I said, not sounding all that friendly.

"Sorry, man. Hey, I forgot to tell you, I spoke to Colleen. She issued an ultimatum. You can go over and get my stuff tomorrow. She gets home a little after eight in the morning, and she's got the day off."

"Tomorrow?"

"Yeah, a little after eight. Otherwise, she's going to burn it. Oh, and you'll probably need a truck."

"A truck?"

"Yeah, there's kind of a lot of stuff. I'll let you go and—" I hung up on him, then quickly put the phone on airplane mode.

"He won't be calling back tonight."

"Promise?"

"Yes, and he doesn't know who you are or where you live."

Her eyes flared but in a positive way. She took a healthy sip, got up off the couch, and turned off the lights. She knelt down in front of the fire on her oriental rug, then said, "Come on down here, it's a lot more comfortable."

Yeah, it was definitely a full moon.

Eight

I put the coffee on for Heidi, kissed her goodbye, and tip-toed out of the house. I pulled into my driveway a little before nine. Morton was on the living room couch and watched me climb out of my car. He started barking the moment my foot hit the front porch. He was jumping against the front door as I tried to open it.

"Morton, what the hell, have you been outside?"

"I guess I kind of forgot," a voice called from somewhere toward the back of the house.

I hurried toward the backdoor with Morton leading the way. The moment I opened the door, he leaped off the back porch and into the yard. I watched him for a very long moment. He lifted his leg against his favorite spot. I walked past a sink full of dirty dishes and into the dining room. Demarcus was painting with his back to the large dining room window.

"Hey, man, how'd the night go?"

"Why are you painting in here?"

"The light's better. I'm just adding highlights, worked on shadows and mid-tones through the night."

"Yeah, well, don't forget to do the dishes in the sink."

"Huh? Oh, yeah, sure thing. Hey, did you give Colleen a call yet?"

"Colleen?"

"Yeah, you were going to get all my stuff from her today, or she's going to burn it in the fire pit she has in the backyard. Oh, and remember, you'll probably need a truck."

"Oh, God. I'm supposed to finish up reviewing a stack of résumés and have them back to my client."

"As soon as you get that stuff, I can move out of here into my own place."

"How large a truck should I get?"

I rented a U-Haul cargo van then hurried over to Colleen's house, ready to do just about anything to get Demarcus out of my hair. He couldn't remember her address although he'd resided there for the past four-plus months. He couldn't call her to get the address because she'd blocked his phone and any online access. I couldn't call her because I'd left my phone somewhere on the oriental rug in front of Heidi's fireplace. Nonetheless, I had the street name, a description of the house, and an approximation of the address.

"It's in the 1700 block of Beechwood Avenue over in Highland Park, a two-story brick joint. Has one of those stupid mailboxes on the front stoop that you have to open with a key. I remember she was all pissed off and bought the thing because she caught me reading her mail one day. Big deal. Not like there was anything interesting. Anyway, you can't miss the place," Demarcus said.

"And you can't recall the address?"

"Yeah, funny thing, my mind seems to be blanking out everything about her. It's why I have to finish this painting of her pretty soon, or I'll forget what she looks like. In case you didn't know, it's a full moon, and I've always enjoyed operating on kind of a lunar calendar. Forty-eight hours from now, I'll be lucky if I even know the name of her street."

I didn't feel the need to tell Demarcus how the lunar calendar seemed to recently be working in my favor. I drove over to the 1700 block of Beechwood, and there, third house from the corner, was number 1721, a two-story Cape-Cod-style house with a free-standing mailbox on the front stoop. The mailbox featured a locked container for mail. I parked in front and rang the doorbell.

A woman with piercing blue eyes and dark hair pulled back in a ponytail answered the door a moment later. She bore an uncanny resemblance to the nude Demarcus had been working on when I left him at my house. "Yes?"

"Colleen Lacy?"

"Yes."

"My name is Dev Haskell. I'm here to get the items belonging to Demarcus Cantrell out of your home."

She glanced over my shoulder at the U-Haul cargo van. "You rented that van?" she said.

"Yeah, he's staying at my place for a couple of days."

She half chuckled, then asked, "How's that working out?"

"In all honesty, it's driving me crazy. I told him he's got to line something up by tomorrow. I have guests coming in at the end of the week," I lied.

"You happen to be preaching to the choir. What did you say your name was, Dan?"

"Dev, short for Devlin."

"Okay, Dev, come on in. I'm so anxious to get rid of this junk I'll even help you haul things out."

"Oh, thanks, but you don't have to do that. I can get it."

"Oh, believe me, it is so not a problem. I just want all that junk out of here so I can begin to get my life back to some semblance of normal. Come on in," she said and held the door open for me.

We walked through the living room and into the dining room, past the wall mural of the naked woman eating the apple while sitting on a dinner platter. The image Demarcus had emailed me didn't do the thing justice. I had to admit, it was pretty good, if you liked that sort of thing in your dining room.

Colleen glanced back at me, saw I had stopped to look at the image and said, "Oh God, there it is, proof positive of the absolute last straw. I was tired, just coming off a double shift, and when I saw this, I just wigged out. Before you say anything, I know, I mean it's good, really good. I just don't want it on my dining room wall. He's so talented. He'd work a month on some exquisite painting and then I'd never see the thing again. I'd ask about it, but he just dodged my questions so many times I quit asking. Then he started doing that paint splatter stuff. I don't think he ever sold one. In fact, I know he didn't because he made a point of telling me almost every day he never sold anything. He'd go on and on about Vincent Van Gogh never selling anything until after he died. God, all it ended up doing was making me want to kill him. That's why I finally told him to leave otherwise, I'd probably be sitting in jail as we speak."

"I agree, it is really good, although the dinner platter isn't exactly my choice."

"Yeah, and that's my mom's china pattern, with a naked woman stretched out on it. God! I'm sure he was thinking it was a personal touch. Of course, I suppose if I left it on the wall, there would never, ever, be a lull in dinner conversation."

I studied the image for another moment. "You know, Colleen, I'm not just saying this, but it's really, really good. The thing should be in the Sistine Chapel, or maybe their lunchroom, if they have one there."

"Yeah, I know. That was the frustrating part. All this talent, he would copy things out of his art books, make them just slightly different. I mean, you'd think they were an original from one of the masters, or something, of course, he never signed them. I'd see the paintings, and then they just disappeared, and what did he end up spending his time on? Those ridiculous paint splatter things. I wanted to scream and, well, finally, I just did.

It's kind of like he's just got this weird, totally bizarre side to the artistic personality."

Nine

Coleen opened up the basement door and said, "Everything is piled up downstairs."

I followed her down into the unfinished basement. A double laundry tub sat in the far corner of the basement, just between a washer and dryer. On the opposite wall was a large chest freezer. Back in a far corner were maybe a dozen boxes stacked two high and a few blank canvases. There was just the slightest hint of a pine scent or maybe turpentine in the air.

"That's all there is? God, I was expecting piles and piles of stuff."

"That's all there is in the house. I've got everything else stacked outside next to the fire pit. I told him if he didn't get everything out of here by the end of the day, I was going to burn it, and I wasn't kidding."

"Well, he took you at your word."

"Can I give you a little advice?" she said.

"Yeah, sure."

"Don't unload any of this at your house, you'll be stuck with it forever. It all starts to become like a nest for him, somehow makes him feel more at home. Hang onto that van overnight and haul everything to wherever it is he lands, then change your locks. And one more thing, don't give him any money. If he hasn't told you yet that he's a little tight on rent money or a down payment, a prescription or something, he will within the next twenty-four hours."

"Sounds like the voice of experience speaking."

"You've had him for a couple of days? Multiply that by four and a half months. And I loved the guy, really, I did. Still do, at least from a distance, but ultimately, it just got to be too much. The mess, all the stuff piled everywhere, rarely in bed together except for maybe fifteen minutes until he was taken care of, then as I was getting up to go to work, he'd be going to sleep. He mention the potential buyers to you yet?"

"Buyers? No, he told me he couldn't sell anything, and looking at all that paint splatter stuff he has, I don't doubt him for a moment."

"I don't know. Calls would come through at crazy hours of the night. He'd be talking to some guy named Maynor or another one named Pascal. He'd hang up the phone with one of those two and suddenly be working on something beautiful, nonstop for two weeks, and then I'd wake up one day, and he was back to doing splatters. God, it drove me absolutely crazy. Come on, let me give you a hand."

We had everything hauled out of Colleen's basement in less than twenty minutes.

"Probably work best if you drive around the block and then down the alley so you can back up close to the garden gate. I'll go open it for you," she said.

I did just that, backing up to the gate. I climbed out of the van, took three steps into the backyard, and stopped.

"Yeah, believe me, I know what you're thinking. Like I said, I was going to set it all on fire if it wasn't out of here by the end of the day."

She was standing amidst piles of boxes, a lot more rolled-up canvases, some of which looked like they'd been tied up for decades, more splatters of paint on a black or blue background, three more easels, plastic bags full of tubes of paint, cans of turpentine. What looked like a garbage bag full of paint rags. A combination CD player and radio that was paint-splattered and sported an aerial that had been snapped off and now maybe just an inch high, rested behind the garbage bag.

"You hauled all this stuff out here yourself?"

"You may soon be experiencing a similar feeling. I just wanted all of this, this junk, out of my home."

I shook my head and started carrying boxes. Some were filled with books, a lot of large coffee table books about famous artists and artwork, all of which made the boxes quite heavy. Some boxes held clothes. Two held pots, and pans. Some boxes I simply didn't want to open and find out what was inside. It took the better part of an hour and a half, but we eventually got everything loaded in the van. I placed the last two boxes in the passenger seat, only because there was nowhere else to put them. The cargo van was stuffed from floor to ceiling.

"God, I really appreciate your help, Colleen. Tell you the truth, I think I would have probably burned this stuff."

"Yeah, the thought certainly crossed my mind more than once, but at the end of the day, it really doesn't matter what we think. It's important to Demarcus, and he'd be devastated if something happened to any of it."

"I'm not sure he would even know."

"Oh, you'd be surprised. Every once in a while, he rummages through things looking for something he probably hasn't thought of for a couple of years, and lo and behold, he finds it."

I pulled out my phone and checked the time. It was almost two in the afternoon. "Could I talk you into some lunch? I'll buy."

"Oh, thanks, but I'm a mess, and I don't want to be seen like this. How about a rain check?"

"We could do that, or I could go down to Cecil's deli and grab some corned beef and bagels and bring them back here."

"Now, that I could do," she said with a smile.

Ten

I was back in twenty minutes with soft bagels, Swiss cheese, corned beef, and coleslaw.

"Oh, you didn't have to get all that but thank you. I just love this, and I'm absolutely famished after hauling all that stuff out of here. Not a complaint, by the way. God, I feel like I'm finally beginning to get my life back on track." As she spoke, she stood at her kitchen counter piling slices of corned beef onto a bagel. She had mustard, mayonnaise, and pickles out on the counter along with two bottles of beer. She dumped a couple of large spoons of coleslaw over the corned beef, placed four pickle slices over the slaw, spread mustard and mayo on the top half of her bagel, then placed the top on the sandwich. The thing sat about four or five inches high.

I did basically the same thing, then pulled out a kitchen stool and sat down next to her.

"So, how'd you and Demarcus ever meet?" I asked and took a large bite. It was delicious.

"I was modeling. I do that on a regular basis, I get fifty percent, and it's a cash payment. He was one of about a dozen students in the class. Most of them weren't much better than drawing stick figures. I think that was as close to a naked woman as some of them had been in a couple of decades, probably the only reason they ponied up twenty-five dollars for the class. But Demarcus, I mean, he was just out of everybody's league, even the teacher. I really don't know what he was doing there. He could have taught the teacher more than a few things."

"He's that good?"

"God, you saw what he did in my dining room and he was just fooling around. He struck up a casual conversation with me as everyone painted, then at the end, he asked if we could link up somewhere so he could finish his painting."

"So, where did you go?"

"First warning flag I ignored, he came here, said there'd been a fire in his building, and he didn't have anywhere to go and could he finish painting me. He even offered to pay me, so I figured, yeah, might as well make a buck."

"So, he paid you?"

"Ahh, no. He worked the entire afternoon, then showed me the painting, and I was so impressed I felt like I had to do something, even though he was going to pay me, so I cooked him dinner. Two bottles of wine later, I wake up with a dreadful headache, and Demarcus has basically moved in."

"You let him stay?"

"Yeah, just about the time I was going to suggest he should maybe think about leaving, he gave me the painting."

"You still have it?"

"Oh yeah, and a couple more that are, well, maybe a little more shall we say, 'revealing.' Anyway, he told me he could sell it for about five grand, but he wanted to give it to me. So, I took it, and the next thing I know, he was moving *'just a couple of things in for a few days.'* Now that I look back, it ended up being about a month of him moving in a couple of things every day."

"You didn't think that was strange?"

"Let's just stop with, 'I didn't think.' What is it you guys always say? You were thinking with the wrong head. It was the female version of that."

"I seem to be in that position a lot."

"Anyway, as nice as he is or can be, it's like he lives two different lives, almost a split personality. He can paint these beautiful figures and scenes. I mean like museum-quality. He cooked dinner, was extremely attentive, very kind, then one day you turn around, and he's splashing paint on a canvas that any five-year-old could do and working all hours, so he's not in bed with me. Meanwhile, the pile of *just a couple of things* kept growing and growing."

"Can I see the painting he did of you?"

"Mmm-mmm, I'll show you one of them, that first one he did. I like them all, but the first one is my favorite. Let me go get it," she said, then slid off her stool and headed out of the kitchen. A moment later, I heard her footsteps heading upstairs. She returned to the kitchen, carefully holding a painting in an elaborate gilt frame.

She stood about five feet away and held the painting toward me. It wasn't large, maybe twelve by eighteen inches, but it really did look like museum-quality. Not that I was any judge, but it was good, very good. Colleen standing naked on some steps in a garden with a pond in front of her, the thing had a real classic quality to it.

"What do you think?" she said.

"You're kidding. Demarcus painted that?"

"Yeah, like I said, the other people in the class were drawing stick figures, and he comes off with this stuff. I mean, even the teacher was speechless. She knew he was way beyond her league. The thing was beautiful after just two and a half hours, and he asks if I would meet up with him sometime, so he could finish it. I'd say all told, he's maybe got seven or eight hours invested in this, which isn't a whole lot of time, considering. I mean, look at it. I couldn't do this in a year."

"You know when he told you it was worth five grand, I thought it was bullshit, but, God, and that background, he just made that up?"

"Yeah, I guess. I mean, we were in a classroom for the first session, and he finished it up in the guest room upstairs. There's just two twin beds and a table lamp in there, nothing like this, not even out the window."

"He was working on something similar the other day. I'm pretty sure it was you he was painting. I asked him about it, and the next thing he's talking about a new frontier or something with those stupid paint splotches. I don't get it. That painting there of you is really cool. Kind of funny, he wouldn't sign the thing."

"Yeah," she said, setting the painting on the counter behind her. "I never got it either. All that talent and he's doing paint splatters. Like I said, it was almost like he has a split personality or something. Hey, you want another beer?"

"You gonna have one?"

"I will. Let me get these plates out of here, and we can have a little dessert."

"I'm not sure I have room."

"Not to worry, it's Rice Krispie bars."

"That I have room for."

We chatted over two more beers and half a pan of Rice Krispie bars. She was really nice, and I could see why Demarcus wanted to move in with her. I just couldn't figure out why he seemed to have a screw loose, and neither could Colleen.

Eleven

Since I already had three beers in me, I figured one more couldn't hurt, so I cruised over to The Spot bar on my way home. My office mate and drinking buddy, Louie Laufen, was already holding court on a corner stool, and Mike was bartending. They were arguing about whether or not salsa and Picante were the same thing. By the way, neither one of them had a drop of Hispanic blood and probably couldn't tell the difference anyway. It sounded like the argument had been going on for at least twenty minutes.

"Well, finally, look what the cat dragged in. Where have you been all day?" Louie said.

"He's probably been peeking in windows like he gets paid to do," Mike said.

"Wrong. If you must know, I've spent the day helping people."

They both laughed.

"No, really. I told Demarcus I needed him out, like by tomorrow."

"And that's helping him?" Louie said.

"Yeah, first of all, he needs to get out of my house and into a place of his own before I kill him."

"Oh, yeah, that sure sounds helpful."

"And he needed a number of things moved out of his former location. Actually, an entire cargo van full of junk. The woman he had been staying with was, literally, at the end of her rope and ready to burn all his stuff. So, I went over there and hauled everything out of her place."

"Why didn't he go?"

"She told him she never, ever wanted to see him again. Blocked his phone and emails and then threatened to burn all his crap if he didn't get it out of her place by tonight."

"That sounds kind of bitchy," Mike said.

"To be honest, I get where she was coming from. I'm at just about the same point. I got that cargo van loaded with nothing but crap, and he had it scattered all over her house. She told me she was just happy to start getting her life back together. To tell you the truth, she was really nice, and Demarcus was just taking advantage of her, well, up until the point where she snapped."

"And now he's at your place?"

"He's out of there as of tomorrow. He's supposed to find a place today, I told him he had to go. She warned me not to unload the cargo van because it would just encourage him to stay."

"So, does he have somewhere to go?"

"I'm about to find out in just a minute," I said, then pulled the phone from my front pocket. "Might be nice

Art Hound ♦ 59

to get a Leinenkugel's poured for me while I make the call and get the good news."

"Coming right up."

"I'll have another one, too. As long as Dev's buying," Louie said, then drained his glass and pushed it across the bar.

The phone rang ten times before it dumped into the message center. "Hi, this is Demarcus. Can't take your call at the moment. Leave a message, and I'll get back to you."

"Demarcus, this is Dev. Calling to see where your new place is located. I got a cargo van loaded up with your stuff. Better plan on not painting tomorrow because we'll be moving all your stuff. Call me."

"He's probably busy going through your cabinets, looking for things he can use in his new place."

"First things first. I have to get him out of my place, and then I'll worry about him taking anything."

"You might want to get your locks changed if you're thinking he'd do something along those lines," Louie said.

"You know, you're the second person to tell me that today," I said, then nodded thanks to Mike and took a sip of my beer.

"Gives one pause to wonder at what point you might start to pay attention?"

I made a mental note about changing the locks, thinking more and more it sounded like some pretty sound advice.

The one beer I had planned on staying for turned into four or five before I climbed back in the cargo van and took the back roads home. I pulled up in front of my place ten minutes later and parked on the street. I was out of the van and headed up the front sidewalk before it dawned on me that the entire house was dark. I actually heard Morton barking before I spotted him standing on the couch watching me through the front window, in the dark.

He continued barking and jumping back and forth as I opened the front door. I turned on the light in the front entry and gave him some heavy-duty scratching behind his ears, then followed him to the backdoor and let him out. He barely made it out the door before he left a rather large deposit right next to the back steps.

"Demarcus, hey, Demarcus," I called, then started turning on lights throughout the first floor. No one answered. I hit the light on the staircase and headed up to the second floor, calling his name as I went, but never got a reply.

I checked the guest room. The bed was unmade. What looked like three or four dirty plates and silverware were piled on top of the dresser. An empty bag of lime-flavored Dorito chips and an empty container of guacamole sat on the floor alongside the bed. I walked to the other side of the bed, noticed that his suitcase was gone, and in its place sat the 4.5-liter bottle of Jameson that I'd hidden under the kitchen sink, now missing a good quarter of its contents. A glass rested on the window sill, empty except for the remnants of a couple of melted ice cubes.

I placed another call to Demarcus and got dropped into his message center again. I left a brief, to-the-point message. "Hey, Demarcus, Dev. Call me, now."

I checked my room, looked under the bed, in the closet, the bathroom. I pulled the shower curtain back. I checked the junk room, the attic, the basement, and then went out and looked around in the garage. Demarcus was nowhere to be found.

Twelve

It was sometime after three in the morning when Morton began to whine and woke me. I rolled over, scratched him behind the ears, and told him to go back to sleep. He quieted down for just a minute or two, then started up again and pushed me with his paw, apparently expecting me to get up and investigate whatever it was he thought he heard.

"Go back to sleep, Morton."

He pushed me again, this time with both front paws. Then he got up on all fours and tried to move me out of bed using his head. He gave no sign of this ending anytime soon, and I figured the poor guy's internal schedule was probably all goofed up because idiot Demarcus apparently hadn't been around to let him outside since God only knew when.

"Okay, okay, I'm up. Happy? Now come on, you want to go outside?"

Morton lowered himself onto the bed.

"Come on, you woke me up. Come on, Morton, outside. Come on, let's go."

Even in the dark, I could see he was staring at me.

"Morton, come on, let's go."

There was a sudden noise that sounded like it was from downstairs, a thud as if something might have fallen over. I opened the bedroom door and glanced back at Morton, who had just shoved his head beneath my pillow. I heard the noise again from downstairs.

Maybe it was Demarcus moving items out to his new place, maybe. I opened the small drawer on the bedside table and pulled out a pistol, slipped my boxers on, and headed toward the staircase. I looked over the banister and down to the first floor. There didn't appear to be a light on anywhere downstairs. If it was Demarcus moving things, he was apparently working in the dark. I was tempted to call out his name, but then decided against it and slowly made my way down the stairs.

I halted, barefoot, wearing only boxers, out in the hallway alongside the living room. I crouched down and waited. It seemed like hours, but it was probably more like two or three minutes. I heard a tearing sound. It was distant, soft, hard to pick up, but it was definitely there. A light flashed on in the den, for a brief moment, no more than a second or two, not the room light, but more like a flashlight of some sort, and then a whispered voice. I couldn't make out what was being said.

I edged my way closer to the den. Now, I could make out two voices, barely, but still couldn't understand what was being said. At this point, I was next to the door and could hear faint thumps and bumps. It sounded like whoever was in there was moving things around. All I could come up with was two kids in there trying to steal my flat screen. Suddenly more whispering. This time I could make it out, two voices again, but it didn't sound like English.

I took a deep breath, held the pistol up in my right hand, and then with my left, reached in the room, and switched on the light. At the same moment I stepped into the room and shouted, "Don't move. You move, and so help me."

I was staring at a large figure, not that he was tall. At least, I was pretty sure it was a he. He was dressed all in black. Shoes, trousers, turtleneck and a black balaclava pulled over his face. He was fat, not just heavy, this guy was fat, with what appeared to be a fairly substantial beer gut. All this to steal a three-year-old flat screen?

I took a couple of steps toward him, holding the pistol upright, making sure he could see the thing and realize I wasn't kidding around. "Just what in the hell do you think you're doing?"

It came out of nowhere. I'm guessing a karate chop of some sort to the back of my neck. My pistol fired up into the ceiling as I went down. Fatty waddled past me and out of the room. I started to slowly get to my feet, shook my head for a moment as I rose on my knees, then got clobbered again, and blacked out for I don't know how long.

As I gradually began to regain consciousness, my first thought was that I'd been dragged onto a beach. It felt like there were all sorts of sand and stones over me.

I slowly rose to my knees, shook my head, and realized I was still in my den. There were dust and chunks of plaster all around, the plaster ceiling had fallen on me. The ceiling where stupid, idiot, jerk Demarcus had let the bathtub overflow must have collapsed when the bullet hit it. I coughed up some plaster dust, slowly got to my feet and looked around. The flat screen was still sitting on the cabinet, and the remote was still on the coffee table, although now they were both covered with chunks of plaster.

I slowly stepped out of the room, looked down the hall, and saw that my front door was open. I stepped out onto my porch and looked around. The front porch light was on, and someone in a taxi drove past and honked at me. I stepped inside, locked the door, then headed back to the kitchen, turning on every light along the way.

My backdoor was wide open, and I pulled it closed. It was then that I noticed a round hole in the glass, not broken, but cut. I opened the door again and looked out on the back stoop. There was a suction cup device lying on the stoop. A round piece of glass with about a six-inch diameter was still attached to the suction cup. I pulled the door closed then locked it. I went back upstairs, got on my cellphone and called 911.

I sat down on the edge of my bed and noticed for the first time that my nose was bleeding, the blood steadily dripping onto my chest.

"Ramsey County Emergency Services."

"Hello, I'm calling to report a break-in and attempted robbery."

"Attempted robbery?"

"Yes, I think there were at least two individuals on the first floor of my home. I confronted them, they assaulted me and ran out the door."

"Are they there now?"

"I don't think so. I locked the doors, but I didn't check outside."

"I'm dispatching a squad as we speak. Do not go outside. Stay in your home until the officers arrive. They'll come to your front door."

"I'm not planning on going anywhere."

"Are you injured?"

"I'm bleeding."

"I'm dispatching a paramedic unit. The squad car has an ETA of three minutes. You are calling from …" She read off my address, and as I was confirming it, I thought I could hear a distant siren.

"I think I can hear the siren."

"Do not open the door until the officers have arrived."

The siren was definitely growing closer.

"All right, I'll wait for them by the door."

"Would you like to remain on the line with me until the officers have arrived?"

"No, thanks, that won't be necessary."

"It's not a problem on this end, sir. I'd be happy to stay here."

"Thanks, but no, really, I'll wait for them downstairs."

"All right, sir. ETA is now about two minutes."

She was wrong. They pulled up about thirty seconds later in front of the U-haul van. I'd barely had a chance to pull on some sweat pants and hurry back downstairs. I watched out the front door. Two cops climbed out of the squad car, big guys, made even bigger-looking by the protective vests they were wearing. Just as they climbed onto the front porch, another squad car pulled in across my driveway just behind the cargo van. An officer got out and then opened his rear door. Out jumped a German shepherd, and both of them headed up my driveway. The dog was on a leash.

"Want some backup?" one of the cops called, just as I opened the front door.

"No worries, I've got the bow-wow," the guy with the dog said and disappeared along the side of the house.

"You okay?" the cop who was just about to knock on the door said to me. He was staring at my still bloody nose and the blood that had dripped onto my chest.

"I'm okay," I said, running my hand across my upper lip, which did nothing to improve things. I was suddenly aware of a throbbing pain along the bridge of my nose.

"Mr. Haskell, is it?"

"Yeah, please, call me Dev."

"Dev, let's have you step back inside. I'm going to just check the exterior. Ian, maybe you'd step inside with

Mister, I mean, Dev. I'll go around the other side. Be back in a few minutes."

The other cop nodded and stepped into the house, closing the door behind him. "Let's get you back to the kitchen, maybe get something on that nose. Looks like you got clobbered there."

"Yeah, come on back this way," I said as I turned to head toward the kitchen.

"Whoa, you got a hell of a gash on the back of that head, too. Paramedics are on their way. We'll want to have them take a look at that."

I felt the back of my head, flinched at the sudden sharp pain, then drew my hand away and saw it was coated with blood. "Head wounds always bleed a lot more than—" I was suddenly dizzy and couldn't really see for a moment, and my head felt like it was buzzing.

Thirteen

The paramedic was dressed in a dark blue uniform with a red fire department patch on his shoulder that read "St. Paul" in the center, then "FIRE" on top and "DEPT." on the bottom. Two other paramedics were standing behind him casually watching. The two cops who'd first arrived were standing off to the side.

"How many fingers are you seeing?" the paramedic asked.

"I see two, and you've got what looks like a tungsten steel wedding band on your ring finger," I said.

"Good, you're coming around. Think you can sit up, Mr. Haskell? You had a pretty nasty fall, there."

"Yeah, yeah, I'm good to go and whoa—"

"Better take your time, your inner balance is out of whack. That blow to the head must have knocked you out."

"Bastards gave me a karate chop to the back of my neck, and then the ceiling fell down on top of me."

"I've got your wound taped up on the back of your head, but that's just a temporary fix. You're going to need a stitch or two back there. Your nose is broken, apparently not for the first time."

"That's because I'm so easy to deal with," I said and heard some chuckles from the guys standing around.

"Maybe just sit there for a moment, we'll let that head get a little more settled, then we're going to help you to your feet."

"I'm okay. I can make it."

"Just humor me. Let's give things a few moments to settle down in that inner ear, stabilize that balance, and then we'll help you up. Turn your head to the right, yeah, and now tilt your head back. Good, okay, just hold that for maybe half a minute and see if it doesn't help."

While I sat on the floor waiting, the two cops left the room and walked down the hall. They were back, just as the paramedics were slowly helping me to my feet. "That ceiling in the other room fell on top of you, Mr., I mean, Dev?"

"Yeah, someone hit me from behind, I think maybe knocked me out for a moment, and then just as I was getting up, boom, the ceiling came down on top of me, and it was lights out."

"I'd say you were awfully lucky. Pretty much the entire ceiling is down. You're fortunate that head wound isn't any worse than it is. You feel able to tell us what happened?"

"We should really get him over to Regions Hospital," the paramedic said. He waited a second or two for a response, but neither cop said anything. Then he gave the nod to another paramedic, and they slowly lifted me up and onto my feet.

"How's that head?"

"A little dizzy standing up."

"Yeah, we better get him down there. You got a shirt or a jacket somewhere we can get for you?"

"There's a fleece jacket hanging over the back of a stool out in the kitchen?"

"I'll get it," one of the cops said and hurried out of the room. He was back a moment later with my black fleece jacket and handed it to the paramedic who, in turn, held it for me while I slipped my arms into the sleeves and zipped it up.

"You a painter, an artist, Dev? I see all those canvasses stacked up leaning next to your backdoor," the cop who'd just fetched the fleece said.

"Me? God, no, well, unless you're talking painting with a roller, I can handle that action. No, all that stuff belongs to a guy I was letting stay here for a couple of days. He's the artist. Demarcus Cantrell. Really talented guy who seems to be wasting his time doing some kind of modern bullshit, all splatters and drips. They were stacked up in the kitchen? The paintings?"

"Yeah, couple of stacks actually, next to the backdoor."

"Can I go back and see?"

"We should really get that head wound taken care of," the paramedic said.

"Let me take your arm and show me," I said to the cop.

He looked at the paramedic, who just shrugged then nodded. The cop held out his arm. I latched on and headed back to the kitchen with him. Everyone else followed us.

Sure enough, a bunch of canvases were neatly stacked in two long piles leaning against the wall next to the backdoor.

"These weren't like this when I came home tonight. I can't believe the two guys who broke in here were after these. I mean, look at them, the paintings. They're all the same horse shit."

"Looks like something one of my kids would do in daycare. Your artist pal sells these things?"

"Not that I'm aware. Who'd waste their money on this crap? Like I said, he's an incredibly talented guy, I mean really he is, then he spends his time on this shit. I don't get it."

"What'd you say his name was?"

"Demarcus Cantrell," I said, looking at the stacks of paintings and trying to make sense of them. "Who in the hell would want that crap bad enough to break into a house? God, all they had to do was knock on the door, and I would have given them away, Demarcus would never know."

"And this Demarcus, he lives with you?"

"That might be too strong a term. He told me he just needed a place to stay for a couple of days. It's been a few more than a couple of days, and I told him yesterday

I had guests coming and needed him out of here tomorrow."

"He seem offended by that?"

"No, not really. In fact, that U-Haul van out front is crammed full of more of his junk that I picked up from a former girlfriend's house today. She did the same thing, told him he had to leave, then gave him an ultimatum about all his stuff. Said she was going to burn it if he didn't pick it up. So I went and got it."

"And it's in that U-Haul out front?"

"Yeah, crammed full. I don't think you'd be able to fit a birthday card in there the thing is so full."

"Where'd this woman live?"

"Over in Highland Park. Nice house. Nice lady, too, for that matter. Demarcus just seems to be one of those guys who doesn't get he's wearing out his welcome. You know the type?"

The cop nodded but didn't say anything.

"Okay, we can deal with the artwork later. Right now, we need to get you down to the hospital and stitched up. We'll have them check out your balance, and take a look at that nose, too," the paramedic said, then took me by the arm and led me back to the front of the house.

"I think we'll give you a gurney ride out to the ambulance," he said.

"How 'bout you just help me walk out there, and I climb in the back under my own power?"

"You sure? These guys would just love to earn their pay, putting you on the gurney and wheeling you out there."

"Yeah, I'm sure."

"Okay, let's go, one foot at a time, no rush. You just take it easy and let me know if you begin to feel the least bit dizzy or queasy."

"I think I'll make it."

We took our time walking out to the ambulance parked alongside the U-Haul cargo van. They rolled the empty gurney into the ambulance, then helped me cautiously step inside. Once in the back of the ambulance, they strapped me onto the gurney, and we headed toward Regions Hospital. I'm guessing the flashing lights were probably going based on the speed it felt we were moving, but I never did hear the siren. I didn't notice it at the time, but the two cops hadn't left the house, and as we drove off, they turned around and went back inside.

Fourteen

It took no more than ten minutes in the ambulance to get from my place down to the ER at Regions Hospital. That included finding a wheelchair, and in short order, one of the paramedics was wheeling me into the ER reception area. After fifteen minutes of answering questions and giving my insurance information, I wheeled myself into the waiting area. The paramedics were gone at this point.

The waiting area was large, with row upon row of blue faux leather chairs. At this hour of the morning, a little after four, the place was sparsely populated. A couple held a little girl with a barking cough on their lap. She seemed to be asleep except when she coughed, which was about every thirty seconds. It was painful just to listen to her.

There was a guy holding what looked like an ice pack over a black eye. The left side of his face was bruised and swollen, and I guessed he might have been in a bar fight, probably not the first from the looks of him.

A woman in a stocking cap and a quilted jacket who looked to be about a hundred and ten years old sat next to someone I presumed was her daughter. The daughter looked to be maybe around sixty years old and was stretched out on the three seats next to her, sound asleep. The daughter was in shorts and a faded black t-shirt touting Mötley Crüe in formerly white letters that had turned grey over the past decade or two.

Some guy in handcuffs sat in the far corner next to a police officer. Neither one looked very happy, but then again, no one looked very happy about being here, let alone at this hour, and that included me.

It was another hour before someone called me. The couple with the little girl and the mother-daughter team had gone in ahead of me. The guy in handcuffs was snoring, and the cop next to him was scanning things on his cellphone. The guy with the ice pack on the bruised face gave a slight groan, then shook his head in disgust when the nurse called out my name.

I half-waved at her when she called my name, climbed out of the wheelchair, and walked over to her. The dizziness from earlier seemed to have left. She looked at me and then back to the wheelchair, seemed to think for a moment, but didn't say anything.

"Mr. Haskell, you're here for some stitches in the back of the head?"

"I guess so."

"Okay, let's get that taken care of so you can get back home. Thanks for waiting. We're a bit light on staff tonight."

"Appreciate you checking me out. To tell you the truth, if the paramedic hadn't been so insistent, I probably wouldn't have come."

"I get that. Not a day goes by when we don't hear some version of it, and it almost always turns out to be a very good idea that folks did come down and have us take a look." I followed her halfway down a long hall. "Just in here," she said, pushing the door open to a small examination room. "Just have a seat, and the doctor will be right with you."

The doctor came into the room carrying a file in a plastic orange folder about five minutes later. She had dark hair, looked to be about my age, and was fairly attractive. She wore blue hospital scrubs and a white lab coat over that. A stethoscope was wrapped around her neck.

"Mr. Haskell?" she asked, stepping into the room and placing the orange folder on a counter. I was sitting on a black plastic chair at the moment. "Why don't you grab a seat on this examination table and we'll take a look at the back of that head. What happened to your nose?" she asked, then moved her head back and forth a few times, studying my nose from a couple of different angles.

"The ceiling in my den fell in on me, some lath and lots of chunks of plaster."

"Oh, ouch," she said. "Were you gutting a room? Are you in the process of restoring an old home?"

"It's an old home, but no, I wasn't doing any work. I had a houseguest who let the bathtub overflow a few days back. I was hoping the plaster might just dry out and stay in place. You can see how well that idea worked. Enough of the ceiling fell so that the whole thing is gonna have to be taken down, and then I'll have to sheetrock it."

"It's always something in an older home. Hmmmmm, the bridge of your nose could use a couple of stitches. Let's see the back of that head."

I half-turned and bent my head down, then felt her hands moving my hair out of the way. "Mmm-mmm, a couple of cuts. You feeling any pain here?" she said, poking around.

"No, not really. I mean, it hurts, but nothing like a sharp pain."

"Can you tell me your phone number?"

I repeated my phone number.

"How about today's date?"

"Not exactly sure, it's either the ninth or the tenth, but I'm not sure which one."

"Good enough. Let's take a look at those eyes." A nurse stepped into the room, and the doctor rattled off a short list of things she was going to need while she took a small penlight out of her pocket and shined it into my right eye. "Can you look up here?" she said, holding a finger about shoulder height. "Now, follow my finger. Good, good. Okay, and now let's do the other eye, same drill."

I followed her finger back and forth.

"Okay, the good news is there doesn't seem to be any concussion. The bad news is, you're going to need a few stitches in the back of your head. I'm going to have to trim your hair around that wound. Then I'm going to give you a local before I stitch you up. I'm also going to give you a couple of self-dissolving stitches on the bridge of that nose."

At that moment, the nurse came back into the room with a metal tray. There was a syringe along with what looked like a pack of curved needles and some button thread. The doctor gave some instructions to the nurse, who pulled some device out of a drawer then stepped behind me.

"Just lower your head, place your chin on your chest," she said and gently pushed my head down. A moment later, I felt the vibration of hair clippers on the back of my head.

"Usually, it costs me about twenty-five bucks for a haircut."

"Well then, this is your lucky day, our haircut prices don't go up in here until after 6:00 am."

The doctor was suddenly behind me, and I felt a couple of pinpricks around the wound as she gave me a local anesthetic. "We'll just let that work its magic for a couple of minutes until you're numb and then get started back there. Let's see that nose again." She examined my nose, moving from side to side, then shot four areas on either side of the bridge of my nose with the anesthetic while I kept my eyes closed. Then she gave some more instructions to the nurse.

A little while later, I was lying on my back on the examining table, and she was putting stitches in the bridge of my nose. I couldn't feel a thing but thought it might be a good idea to keep my eyes closed all the same. Once she finished, she placed some items in a metal tray, then had me turn over, and she began to stitch up the back of my head.

She was just in the process of finishing up when a familiar male voice suddenly called from behind. "If you're looking for a brain, I can save you the trouble, Doc, there isn't one. There's nothing in there but empty space."

Fifteen

The doctor just laughed and said, "Fortunately, Lieutenant, Mr. Haskell has a pretty hard head."

"More like a very thick skull," Aaron LaZelle said.

We'd known one another since we were kids, and as a lieutenant on the police force and now heading up the city's Homicide division, he'd pulled my feet away from the fire uncountable times.

"Hey, Aaron, what are you doing down here?"

"Please hold still, Mr. Haskell. We're almost done here," the doctor said, then gently pushed my head back down into the circular cushion where it had been.

"Hi, Dev. Amazing finding you in here. Not. Just down checking on one of our fellows injured in a car accident and saw your name on a list of potential troublemakers. Thought I'd better stop in and check things out, see if an arrest or maybe a night in detox might be in order. What happened?"

"Thanks for showing your sensitive and caring side. Like I told the doc, here, I had a house guest who let the bathtub overflow a couple of days ago. I knew the ceiling got soaked, but I was hoping if it dried out, it might be okay. You can see the result of that thought process."

"Nice job. Once again, left to your own devices, you've somehow managed to create a disaster."

"Nothing a few stitches won't cure. He's lucky, there doesn't seem to be a concussion," the doctor said, then stepped away and placed something in the metal tray. "Okay, Mr. Haskell, you can go ahead and sit up. But slowly, we don't want that dizziness coming back. Any headaches, dizziness, or vision problems, I want you to contact us. Some Tylenol over the course of the day should suffice, as far as any pain medication you need," she said, then pulled off her blue latex gloves and tossed them in the wastebasket. "That about does it for today. Sorry, but I don't think that particular hairstyle is going to catch on anytime soon."

"Oh, I don't know. Once everyone sees that it's me wearing it, you might end up with a line out the door wanting you to do the same number on them."

"Well, we're not going to hold our breath. That about does it. You're free to go. If I were you, I'd maybe stick to just showers or shallow baths for the time being," she said and laughed.

"Yeah, thanks. My houseguest is in the process of leaving later today or tomorrow, so that should put an end to a number of my problems. Thanks again for taking care of me, Doc."

"Maybe just sit there for a couple of minutes and take your time walking out. I can get you a wheelchair if you like."

"No, thanks, but it's not necessary."

"You gonna need a ride home?" Aaron asked.

"Actually, yeah, if you can spare the time, that would be great."

"Oh, for you, Dev, I'll make the time. Let me just call my driver and he can pick us up."

"You've got a driver? Gee, nice to see my tax dollars at work."

Aaron just flashed me an all-knowing smile, pulled his cellphone out of his pocket, and put it up to his ear as he walked out into the hallway.

Sixteen

Aaron stepped back into the examination room about ten minutes later. "That doctor says you're a lucky guy. You could have really ended up with your head cracked open."

"God, it knocked me out for a bit. Might have been a minute or ten minutes, I just don't know."

"Well, glad I ran into you. We'll give you a lift home. Driver's just leaving now. It'll take about five minutes to get here. Let's head out to the door. He can pick us up right at curbside."

"How's your guy doing?"

"My guy?"

"Yeah, you said someone was in a car accident. How's he doing?"

"Oh, yeah, they're going to keep him overnight, just for observation. He's not too happy about it, but that's the way it goes. I need him to get a clean bill of health and an okay from the doctor before he goes back out there. Come on, let's head toward the front door. You sure you don't want a wheelchair?"

"You know, the thought of your VIP hands wheeling me around the corridor here is appealing, but I think I'll take a pass."

We walked slowly down the hall, down another hall and turned a corner, then walked another twenty feet before we came to the main corridor. Just as we walked past the information desk and approached the doors leading outside, a black and white squad car pulled up alongside the curb.

"How's that for perfect timing? Come on," Aaron said.

I followed him outside. He opened the rear door of the squad car for me. There were no handles on the inside of the door, and there was a heavy mesh screen between the front and backseat, which I expected.

I started to lean into the backseat, said "Hi," to the driver just as he turned around with a smile on his face and gave me the cold eye stare. I was back out on the sidewalk in half a second.

Detective Norris Manning. The guy hated me and had spent a good deal of his professional and private life trying to get me linked to any and every major crime that had happened in the city over the past fifteen years. He was anything but a friend. Had promised on more than one occasion to put me away for life, and now I was supposed to get in the car with him?

"You've gotta be kidding me. Manning is your driver?"

"Get in. We can talk about it on the way."

"This is a setup, isn't it? You're full of shit. You didn't have anyone injured in a car accident, did you?"

"Dev, if you'll just get in."

"What the hell? You didn't happen to see my name on a list. You came here looking for me. 'Make time to give me a ride home,' that's bullshit. Who are you kidding?"

"Will you just get in the car, Dev? We can talk about it on the way, okay?"

"Talk about it on the way to where? You're not taking me home, are you? You never even planned to."

"We're going to take you home, there just might be a little detour along the way is all, so just get in."

"Make sure you keep Manning on a leash, Aaron. I don't want him anywhere near me. Okay?"

"Okay, okay. Now, will you just get your ass in the damn car and stop making a scene? Please."

"Just keep him away from me," I said and climbed into the backseat. Aaron slammed the door closed and climbed into the passenger seat.

"How's it going, Haskell?" Manning said, turning around and smiling. It looked like he had an evil trick up his sleeve, and he just couldn't wait to pull it on me. He cracked the eternally present piece of gum, switched a toothpick from the right to the left side of his mouth, and stared at me with those cold blue eyes of his. His bald pink head seemed to cast a reflection from the overhead light onto the ceiling of the car.

"Turn around and let's get moving," Aaron said to him.

Manning shrugged, gave me one more evil look and said, "Okay, Haskell, if that's the way you want it." He took his foot off the brake, and we pulled away from the curb.

Once Manning pulled out onto the street, Aaron turned around in the passenger seat and looked at me through the wire mesh screen. "Here's the deal, Dev. We're working on something that happened last night, and your name came up."

"Imagine," Manning chuckled.

Aaron gave him a look for a long moment and said, "Better just watch the road," then turned to face me again. "Tell me what you know about Demarcus Cantrell. This will all be strictly off the record."

"First of all, anything I say will not be off the record. You'll use it in some way, shape, or form."

Manning nodded.

"Dev, you haven't been arrested here. I'm not going to charge you with anything."

"I've a good mind to have my attorney present before I say a word. How do you think it will go down when I file a lawsuit because you and 'Detective Guilty as Charged' there get accused of abducting me from the hospital? Besides, I'm suffering from a recent head wound, and I can't remember anything anyway."

"Well, if that's the way you want to play it, I suppose we can take you home. Of course, that's going to force my hand, and you're liable to be charged with aiding and abetting a fugitive, participating in a kidnapping, involvement in an art forgery ring… you want me to go on? Feel like calling your lawyer? Is he still that guy you office with, Louie Laufen? He won't even answer your phone calls until after the noon hour."

"Kidnapping?"

"Just tell me about Demarcus Cantrell."

"Will we share information?"

"What?"

"Aaron, if something is coming down the pike at me, I need to know. Can we share information? Come on, I've neither the time nor the inclination to get involved in your investigation, well, other than to help by sharing whatever information I have, which will probably bring your investigation to a speedy conclusion. You know, I always like to help. I just don't want to be blindsided here. I had two guys break into my place last night they beat me up and threatened to kill me."

"You told the officers they just gave you a karate chop on the back of the neck that knocked you out. Then the ceiling collapsed on you, interesting timing, by the way."

"How'd you know all that?"

"It's my job."

"So, are we going to share?"

Manning shook his head. Aaron seemed to think for a long moment, then finally said, "God, okay. But I want your word you will, in no way, attempt to shape or insert yourself into this investigation. We've got a woman missing out there, and the first priority is to get her back safe and sound. The best way for that to be accomplished is for you to stay the hell out of it. Clear?"

"Yeah, it's what I wanted all along."

Aaron rolled his eyes, then said, "Okay, so what can you tell me?"

Seventeen

Aaron examined me through the wire mesh for a moment. "First off, who's the missing woman? Don't tell me it's Heidi?" he said as he read my facial reaction.

"Aaron, is Heidi missing, Heidi Bauer?"

"You mean that hot number with the different hair color every time I see her? The woman who makes all that dough investing or running hedge funds or whatever she does? The woman who, unlike every other woman in town, hasn't quite given up on you? That Heidi?"

"Aaron, is she okay?"

"Yeah, as far as I know. I mean, I think she should have her head examined for still letting you in her bed, but yeah, she's fine."

"If it's that Stacy chick, I haven't seen her since she dumped all my stuff on the front porch and spray-painted that graffiti on the side of my car a number of months back."

"Who could blame her? And you could never prove it was her attacking your car, anyway."

"I know it was her. That nutcase Margo? She dumped me. God, I was afraid she was going to stab me the other night. I went over to her place and ended up fleeing the scene."

"You know a woman named Colleen Lacy?"

"Colleen? You're kidding?"

"Dev, do you know her?"

"Yes and no."

"Oh, please, do explain."

At this point, Manning picked up a little speed to make a yellow light. The thing turned red midway across the intersection. The car behind us followed suit, completely running the red light. The driver must have been from Chicago.

"Colleen Lacy. Well, she and Demarcus Cantrell were an item for a couple of months, maybe four or five. She eventually got fed up with his mess and his general pain-in-the-ass behavior and kicked him out. I knew of her, from what Demarcus told me, but I'd never met her until yesterday when I hauled all his stuff out of her place. That was the first time I ever saw her in person. She was nice, very nice, helped me load up the van, and said she was just glad to get rid of all the junk. Then I ran to Cecil's deli and got some corned beef and bagels, we had a late lunch at her place, chatted, and I went home."

"Was Cantrell with you, helping you move his belongings?"

"No, she told him she didn't want to see him ever again. She blocked his phone number and any online access, I guess. Of course, that was his excuse. I think she would have been okay if he was there to haul things out of her place. But it was a convenient excuse he used to avoid a few hours of labor. Jesus, between the two of us, Colleen and me, we filled up the van. It took us over three hours."

"You go straight home?"

"Yeah, well, almost. I mean, I stopped at The Spot for a couple of minutes."

"What time did you get home?"

"Oh, I don't know, I guess, around ten, maybe a little later."

"What time did you go into The Spot?"

"Five-ish," I said, fudging my answer.

Aaron shook his head. "You get up close and personal with her?"

"You mean like *real* up close? No, not that I wouldn't have enjoyed it."

"Maybe you're losing your touch. She mention anything about Cantrell?"

"Well, yeah, I mean, he was the reason I was there, at her place, to begin with. We were both sick of the guy."

"How so?"

"Oh look, he's nice enough, but the mess starts in a corner and slowly begins to spread throughout the entire house. He's apparently short on money, is extremely talented with his painting, but wastes his time painting stuff that a five-year-old could do. I think he means well, but in very short order, he becomes a real pain in the ass. He was at my place for less than a week, and I ended up giving him an ultimatum that he had to leave in forty-eight hours, either today or tomorrow. Colleen had the guy leeching off her for four or five months. She's way more patient than me. It's why she finally got so frustrated she kicked him out. The guy couldn't even be bothered to let Morton out the backdoor."

"Any ideas where he might be now?"

"Cantrell? My best guess would be my place unless he got a burr under his butt and decided to start moving some of his shit to wherever he landed. I told him he had to find somewhere else. To tell you the truth, I'm expecting some kind of stupid excuse from him."

"Well, he hasn't been to your place."

"What? Now you're watching my house?"

"Dev, you were burglarized three or four hours ago. You said yourself they assaulted you, knocked you out. What did they give you, ten or twelve stitches? Yeah, we're watching your house. Trying to keep you safe, and now you're complaining. I don't know, we're only trying to help, and this is the thanks we get?"

"I didn't mean it like that, exactly."

"One would think you'd be a little more grateful."

"You said forgery, earlier?"

Manning had just pulled to the curb in front of Colleen's house. There were two squad cars already parked in front, a crime scene van and two more cars that looked normal enough, but had "cop" written all over them; no whitewall tires, a searchlight mounted on the driver's side, and a pretty heavy-duty radio set into the dash.

"Come on in, and you can show us what you were up to yesterday," Aaron said, then climbed out of the passenger seat. He stepped over and opened the rear door for me.

I groaned as I climbed out. "So, what's going on with everyone here? Is Colleen okay?"

"We don't know. A neighbor across the alley just happened to see her being hustled into a car last night, late last night around midnight by two guys, and called us."

"Maybe friends?"

"They tossed her into the trunk of a black Mercedes. Does that sound like friends to you?"

"Were these guys dressed all in black and one of them was fat, real fat? Cause those were the two idiots at my house."

"That more or less fits the general description. The neighbor lady couldn't really say. It all happened so fast, she was only half awake, and they drove off."

"It was well after midnight when they were at my place."

"The neighbor's call came through around midnight. Maybe this Lacy woman told them about your place, and they headed over."

"I only just met her yesterday. She didn't even know where I lived."

"Yeah, but she had your name, maybe mentioned the U-Haul van. It's parked right in front on the street. Wouldn't be too hard to figure it out."

"Seems like a lot of trouble to get a bunch of horse shit paintings. I mean, she showed me a gorgeous painting that she kept upstairs somewhere, her standing in front of this pond. But the rest of his stuff? I would have helped haul the paintings out to their car if those guys wanted them. Any word on Demarcus in all this?"

"No, at least not as of yet. Just now, the more pressing issue is Colleen Lacy. I'm hoping your pal Demarcus will wash up on shore somewhere this morning, and we can talk to him. Come on, let's go inside and have you take a look."

Eighteen

Once inside, everything looked normal enough. Three or four plainclothes guys were talking in hushed tones in the corner of Colleen's living room. There was a guy photographing the dining room. He shot a good half-dozen images of the naked lady eating an apple that Demarcus had painted on the dining room wall. From the dining room, I could see into the kitchen where some guy was dusting a glass on the counter for fingerprints. No one was wearing hazmat suits, but everyone had on a pair of blue, latex gloves.

The guy photographing the dining room artwork stepped back and gave Aaron a nod, then glanced at me and said, "Nice haircut. You pay extra for that?"

"You get a deal down at the ER if they do it before six in the morning."

"Yeah, I'll bet," he laughed, then headed into the kitchen.

Aaron pulled an extra pair of gloves from his suit coat pocket and handed them to me.

"Here, you better put these on."

"Thanks, although my fingerprints are all over the kitchen and down in the basement. Demarcus had a pile of stuff down there."

"Enough to fill that U-Haul cargo van?"

I made a mental note. It was the second time he'd referred to the van. I'd mentioned the van to Aaron, but only in general terms. I didn't think I ever mentioned I'd rented it from U-Haul. Then again, if there were cops still at my place, there was a pretty good chance Aaron had been there, too.

"Well, we definitely filled up the cargo van, but Colleen already had most of his stuff stacked up out in the backyard next to the fire pit. She'd told Demarcus if he didn't get his stuff out of here by last night, she was going to burn it. All of it."

"How'd he react to that?"

"Well, he conned me into moving it, but as far as I know, he never made an effort to contact Colleen directly."

"Of course you said she had his phone blocked and he couldn't email her. Right?"

"Yeah, true," I said. "But how about leaving a polite note on the door or something? Kind of funny, the guy was camped out here for four months, and he didn't remember the address, just told me it was the third house from the corner, and then described that mailbox on the front stoop. Which, I hasten to add, she told me she got because she caught him reading her mail. She put up with a lot of shit over the course of four months."

"He ever appear violent to you?"

"Demarcus? No, in fact, almost the opposite. Nothing ever really seemed to faze him on an emotional level. When she blocked his calls and stuff, he just kind of let it go like it was no big deal. When he overflowed the tub that ultimately ended up collapsing the ceiling in my den, he just shrugged and maybe said sorry as an afterthought. Is he capable of violence? Yeah, maybe, I suppose. But aren't we all?"

"Some more than others. What do you think about this?" Aaron said and nodded toward the fat lady eating the apple.

"What do I think? Well, a couple of things. It's good, very good. That said I know Colleen wasn't too thrilled. I mean, he just did it and never told her he was going to do it, never asked her permission. I guess the pattern on that china platter is from her mom's china. He did a couple of paintings of Colleen. They should be upstairs somewhere. I saw one of them, absolute museum quality, but instead of doing that kind of work, he was busy painting this just shitty contemporary junk that any five-year-old could do and then wondered why they weren't selling. I mean, it's crazy."

Aaron seemed to think about that for a long moment while looking at the mural on the dining room wall, then said, "Come on, I want to show you something up on the second floor." I followed him out of the dining room and up the stairs.

Nineteen

The steps on the staircase were carpeted in a light beige carpeting. There was a bathroom at the top of the stairs with a bedroom on either side of the bathroom. The same light beige carpeting was in both bedrooms. One of the bedrooms had two twin beds with an end table and a lamp between the beds. The other bedroom was slightly larger and held a king-size bed with an elaborately carved wooden headboard and an upholstered bench at the foot of the bed. What looked like the jeans and blouse Colleen had worn yesterday appeared to have been tossed on the bench. A thong and bra, along with the shoes she'd worn, were on the floor next to the bed.

"I'm pretty sure those are the clothes she wore yesterday," I said.

Aaron nodded, and said, "Check this out," then stepped over to the closet and opened the door. I stepped behind him as he reached up and pulled the cord that turned the closet light on. "Look familiar?" he said.

Hanging directly in front of us was the painting in the gilt frame Colleen had shown me yesterday. It was perfectly centered on the wall and purposely hung in that exact spot, not just resting on a clothes hook or an available nail. Colleen standing naked in a garden with a pond. The painting she'd posed for in the class when she'd first met Demarcus.

"Recognize it?" Aaron asked.

"Yeah, of course, this is the painting Colleen showed me yesterday. She told me she kept it upstairs, but I had no idea it was hanging in a closet. It's definitely her." I went on to tell Aaron how they'd met in the painting class, she and Demarcus, that he'd asked to have her pose again so he could finish the painting and then ended up moving in with her.

"You like the painting?"

"Yeah, I mean, I think it's great. Look at the talent the guy has. You know, she told me it only took him something like eight hours from start to finish to paint that. God, I have a tough time just staying in the lines when coloring with crayons."

"Yeah, it's a copy of an impressionist work, Bather Standing or Standing Bather, I can't remember which. Painted by one Pierre-Auguste Renoir back in 1896," Aaron said, all the while staring at the painting.

"Pretty damn good if you ask me. I guess he more or less did the background from memory once he painted her figure, at least that's what she told me."

"What do you think about these two?" Aaron said, then pushed the blouses and dresses back that were hanging on either side of the closet, revealing two similar paintings. Both were unframed, but they were definitely naked Colleen, only in one of the paintings she was standing in water up to her knees, and in the other, she was sitting on a stone or something and appeared to be drying herself off with a towel.

"Oh, man. What do I think? I think they're very nice. But why would she keep these in the closet? Are they gonna fade in the sunlight or something? I mean, she's beautiful. She poses naked for art classes, so I'm guessing the no clothes thing can't be an issue, at least I don't think it is."

"Amazingly, the original of that first painting, the one with the frame. It's hanging in the Musée d'Orsay."

"No shit? Where's that?"

Aaron glanced at me for a brief moment then said, "Paris, Dev. It's kind of a famous place. Been hanging there for years, or at least it was, up until about two months ago when the museum discovered someone had stolen the original and replaced it with a copy."

"A copy?"

"Yeah, and a damn good one. It had even been painted on hundred-and-fifty-year-old canvas. The forgery was so good they're not even sure when the original was stolen. Could have been up to a year earlier. I guess they do an assessment annually, and that's when they caught it, the fake."

"They think Demarcus painted it?"

"I don't know if I'd go that far. Let's just say the original painting hasn't been recovered, and they're interested enough that they're sending someone over here to check these three out. They've asked us not to touch this one in the frame, or the other two for that matter. Seems to be a strong possibility your friend Demarcus might just be a rather accomplished forger."

"A forger? You gotta be kidding me. I wonder if that's why he didn't sign anything he painted. Aaron, this isn't making sense. I mean, the junk he painted at my place, it's crap."

"I know, I've seen it. It's not adding up to me, either."

"Just for the sake of discussion, what's one of those originals worth? Who did you say the painter was, Reynolds?"

Aaron shot another quick look in my direction and shook his head. "No, idiot, not Reynolds, Renoir. Pierre-Auguste Renoir. French painter, who helped lead the charge in the whole Impressionist movement. He had a painting that went for something like thirty-two thousand back in 2014 and another one back in 1990 that went for seventy-eight-point-one million. It was purchased by some Japanese collector, and became one of the most expensive artworks ever sold."

"Seventy-eight million? For a painting?"

"Seventy-eight-point-one million," Aaron said, reaching up and turning the closet light off.

"God, how big was the thing? It must have been huge."

He looked like he was going to comment but then decided against it, and I followed him back downstairs and into the kitchen.

"Anything, Jamie?" he asked the guy dusting for fingerprints. He'd finished with the glass on the kitchen counter. I looked at it. I didn't think it was the glass I'd drank my beers out of yesterday, and besides, that wouldn't make sense sitting alone on the kitchen counter.

"I think the plates and glasses we had our late lunch on are probably in the dishwasher there. That glass on the counter isn't the one I used."

"We'll know soon enough," Jamie said.

The backdoor window had a circular hole cut into it, large enough so someone could just reach in and undo the lock on the door. It looked very similar to the hole that had been cut in the window of my backdoor.

"That hole in the door—"

"Is just like the one on your door. Yeah, we know," Aaron said.

"Did you guys get the suction cup thing that was lying on my back steps?"

"Bagged and tagged," Aaron said. "It's one of the reasons I wanted you here. I'd like to review your descriptions."

"Oh, God," I groaned. "Does that mean I have to go down to headquarters and sit in one of those rooms where my blood pressure will skyrocket, and Manning will ask stupid questions? Where is he, by the way?"

"Why? Miss him?"

"Are you kidding?"

"He's waiting for us out in the car. Let's get you back to your place, and you can bring me current on Demarcus. Be nice to know where he is."

"That, I don't know."

"Maybe you can help us find out. Come on. I wouldn't want to keep you from your much-needed rest."

Twenty

Mercifully Manning didn't so much as utter a word during the entire drive, all twelve minutes. He rounded the final corner, drove a block, then suddenly cranked the wheel sharply and sped up my driveway. He screeched to a stop about a half-inch behind my car. He turned with an evil grin and said, "We're here."

"You know, Manning, anyone ever tell you, you're one great big—"

"Come on, save it, you two. Let's go," Aaron said and jumped out. He opened the rear door so I could climb out. Manning just sat behind the wheel and didn't make an effort to move. I noticed there was just one squad car parked out front along with the U-Haul van, but nothing else that looked like an official vehicle. We climbed the front porch steps and went inside. Aaron walked into the front entry hall and looked around, taking in the view. I casually locked the front door once inside just in case Manning followed so he'd have to ring the doorbell. I heard footsteps coming our way from the kitchen.

"Tell me what happened," Aaron said.

"Not much to it. I heard a noise a little after three. Actually, Morton heard it and woke me. It sounded like a soft thump. I didn't pay much attention, figured it maybe came from outside, well, until I heard it a second time. I tiptoed downstairs, crouched down right there." I pointed to the wall a few feet away from the door to my den.

"You see them?"

"Not from there. I actually heard them whispering, but I couldn't make out what they were saying. Tell you the truth, I don't think they were speaking English. Might have been French or Spanish. Anyway, I figured some kids were maybe trying to steal my flat screen, but the thing's three years old, so that didn't seem to make a lot of sense."

A cop suddenly stepped into the living room. She was Asian, very pretty, and I immediately recognized her. Lin Nguyen. "Lieutenant," she said and nodded at Aaron. "And you must be Mr. Haskell. I'm Officer Lin Nguyen." She flared her eyes as she spoke, and I took that to mean I shouldn't indicate our past involvement.

"Nice to meet you, Officer," I said and nodded back. The last time I'd seen her was in my kitchen, maybe a year or two ago. She'd just finished telling me things didn't seem to be working out, kissed me on the cheek, and walked out the door. She'd left some red silk undergarments beneath a pillow in my bedroom, and I'd always hoped it was a sign she might come back, but that had never happened, at least until now, and this didn't really count.

"You don't think they were speaking English?" Aaron said.

"What? Oh, yeah, see, they were whispering. At first, I thought it might be some kids trying to steal my flat screen, but that didn't seem to make much sense. So, I reached into the room, turned on the light, and there's this fat guy all dressed in black with a balaclava pulled over his face looking back at me. Next thing I know some bastard gives me a karate chop to the back of my neck, I hit the floor, and that's when the damn ceiling fell on top of me."

"I'm guessing you failed to mention you were carrying a gun." By this point, Aaron had stepped up to the doorway into the den and was staring up at the exposed lath work on the ceiling.

Lin smiled and looked the other way until she could stop laughing.

"A gun? No, I was carrying cupcakes, I wanted to welcome them into my home at three in the morning. Yeah, I had a gun. If I knew how things were going to work out, I would have rolled a grenade into the room."

Aaron took a couple of steps into the den and looked around. "I don't know if a grenade could have done much more damage. Show me how you turned on the light in here."

I stepped over to the doorway, reached in, and flipped on the light switch. "Pretty much like that. When

I was crouched out in the hall trying to figure out what was going on, there was a light for just a few seconds. I'm guessing it was a flashlight of some sort. I didn't realize they were stacking all of Demarcus's canvases by the backdoor. Apparently, they were planning on taking the things. God knows why, they're absolutely awful."

"And the guy who hit you?"

"He must have been somewhere over there." I pointed to a burgundy upholstered chair with a leopard skin fleece blanket folded over the back. "I was so focused on the fat guy I never even saw him. The whole thing from me stepping into the room to them running out the front door maybe took three to five seconds."

"The fat guy say anything?"

"Not that I can recall. But like I said, I got clobbered from behind almost immediately."

Aaron walked past me and headed for the kitchen. "And your dog, he didn't bark or growl or anything."

"No, he woke me up, then hid his head under the pillow."

"Nice protection," he said as we stepped into the kitchen.

Demarcus's paintings were lined up in two neat stacks next to the kitchen door. The door was closed, but the circular hole where they'd cut the glass to get in was clearly visible.

"Same as Colleen Lacy's," Aaron said. "It's either the same guys or one hell of a coincidence. And these are his paintings, Demarcus Cantrell?"

"Yeah. See what I mean? You could do them all in an afternoon with one hand while pounding down beers with the other. Absolutely dreadful, just look at the damn things."

"You'll get no argument from me. And then you've got those masterpieces she had virtually hidden in the closet," he said, shaking his head. He turned and looked at me. "Sorry to admit it, but you're right, it doesn't make any sense."

Aaron got a phone call and left maybe five minutes later. On his way out the door, he told Officer Lin she could leave.

I watched out the front door as Manning backed out of my driveway. He seemed to make a point of keeping one set of wheels on the grass all the way down the driveway, then backed across the corner of my boulevard, leaving a tire tread on the grass. I know he did it on purpose because he smiled at me and waved before he put the car in drive and took off with the siren going and the lights flashing.

"You going to be okay here on your own, Dev?" Lin asked.

"Yeah, I'm just," I thought for a second. "Well, actually, I think I'll be okay, maybe. Got this head wound when they hit me over the head with the pistol."

"I thought you said the guy you never saw gave you a karate chop to the back of your neck."

"Yeah, umm, he did that, then I think he hit me over the head with a pistol, 357 Magnum or something. Big, whatever it was. Got something like thirty or forty stitches. They wanted to keep me in the hospital for a couple of days, but I want to get on this case right away. The last thing I need is giving these guys another two days to clear out of town."

"Do you want me to stay with you?"

"I'd love it, but you better go. Don't know if I could trust myself, you know?"

She smiled at that and nodded. "How 'bout I give a call and check in at the end of the day? Just to make sure you're okay."

"I think that would probably be a pretty good idea."

Twenty-one

Lin left with the promise to check in on me at the end of the day. I had a lot to do in the interim. I changed the sheets on my bed, bought some wine, stole flowers from the neighbor's garden, and put them on the dining room table and in the kitchen. I bought two steaks, grabbed a Big Mac, and screwed a piece of plywood over the window in the backdoor. Then, against my better judgment, I hauled all of Demarcus's junk out of the U-Haul van and into the house, returned the van, and last, but not least, put two stemmed glasses in the freezer just on the odd chance Lin was in one of her martini moods.

I was just settling onto the kitchen stool and in the process of unwrapping a Snickers bar when Lin called a little after four.

"Hey, how's that head?"

"Oh, it's definitely still there. Bit dizzy. The pain has moved down into my shoulders. My neck is getting stiff and, well, the headache seems to have gotten worse. I don't know, I—"

"Oh, you poor thing. I don't suppose you called your doctor?"

"Actually, I did, but they can't get me in until late tomorrow," I lied. "He said something about stress relief, but I don't have that kind of time. Guess I'll just have to suffer through, and hopefully, tomorrow things will be a little bit better, maybe, I hope."

"Oh, God, that doesn't sound like much of a plan. Have you had anything to eat today?"

"Tell you the truth. I just didn't feel like eating. Now that you mention it, I haven't had anything. Not so much as a bite all day," I said, setting the Snickers bar on the kitchen counter.

"You want me to come over? I could give you a shoulder rub, or a back rub, hopefully, get you relaxed."

"Oh, you don't have to do that, Lin. That's really sweet of you, but I don't want to impose. Besides, I know it was probably more than a little uncomfortable for you having to sit around here this morning after, well, you know."

"Don't worry about that. Right now, the important thing is to get you relaxed and on the mend. How about I swing by tonight, say half-past six. I promise I'll be nice, very nice."

Yes, yes, yes. "Well, if you're sure it won't be an imposition. I don't want to screw up your personal life or any plans you had for tonight."

"Believe me, nothing's happening on that end, so there isn't anything to screw up. I'll bring some dinner for you to eat."

"No, I tell you what, let me at least make you dinner. You're such a sweetheart, I know you'd rather be somewhere else, and I really appreciate you going the extra mile for me."

"Actually, there's nowhere I'd rather be tonight. I'll see you in a bit. You just take it easy until I get there. Okay?"

"Okay. Thanks again, Lin."

I figured I'd better take Morton for a long walk so he'd calm down for the evening and not screw things up. I got his leash, and we did at least a couple of miles. I ate a half-dozen chocolate chip cookies when we returned, then hit the shower, shaved, and put some clean clothes on. I was just heading downstairs and into the kitchen when my doorbell rang.

Twenty-two

I opened the door and grinned. "Hey, Lin, thanks. It's so kind of you to come over."

"How are you doing?" she asked, then shifted the brown paper grocery bag in her arms, and I heard bottles clink. She leaned forward and planted a long, lingering kiss on my cheek.

"Here, let me take that bag from you," I said just as Morton wandered over and shoved his nose between her legs.

"Oh, hi, Morton. Some things never change," she said and laughed.

"Can't really blame him. Come on back to the kitchen," I said and headed back.

She paused for just a moment and seemed to make a mental note of all the stuff piled in the living room. "Is it just me or do you seem to have a lot more of that guy's junk in here? What was his name, Demento?"

"Close, Demarcus. I had to unload the van and get that returned, so I dumped everything in the living room. Not fun, let me tell you. It was really hard. Had to sit down a number of times until the dizziness passed."

"God, Dev, you should have called, I would have emptied the van for you. How's that head? Did you say you got thirty stitches?"

"Yeah, thirty or forty, I can't quite remember. They said most of them are the self-dissolving kind. Told me I was lucky I got into the ER when I did. I wasn't too wild about going, but the paramedics insisted, and to tell you the truth, I'm glad they did. Course, now that pain seems to have gone down to my shoulders and back." I grimaced and rolled my shoulders for effect.

"Oh, you poor thing. Well, here, doctor's orders." She took the bag from me and set it on the kitchen counter. "As of now, I'm in charge, and I don't want to hear another word, or you'll get a spanking," she said and raised an eyebrow. "You just sit down there at the kitchen counter and let me pour you a glass of wine."

"Lin, you don't have to do that."

She reached up, kissed me on the lips, and whispered, "Poor baby. Those eyes are looking black from that broken nose. Did they straighten it out? It doesn't seem to have a curve in it," she said, moving her head from side to side, studying my nose for a long moment before she gave me another kiss.

I could feel my recovery suddenly moving into full swing.

She prepared our dinner, steaks with mushrooms and onions, baked potatoes, steamed broccoli, and ciabatta rolls while I continued my recovery with a second glass of wine.

We were finishing our meal. I had just a couple of bites of steak left on my plate and was planning to eat them once I worked my way through the broccoli when the doorbell rang. It was almost eight.

"Who the hell could that be?"

"Just leave it," Lin said. "Probably someone wanting you to pledge funds or something."

"I better check. If it's a kid selling stuff, I always feel like I should buy."

"Oh, you're so sweet," she said, then took another sip of her wine as I headed toward the front door. Morton remained in the kitchen with Lin and the steak.

It looked like a delivery guy out on the front porch. He was dressed in a dark blue shirt and trousers. He was holding a box in front of him. I could just make out the top of a dark blue baseball cap on his head.

"Yes?" I said as I opened the door.

"Mr. Haskell?"

"Yeah."

"Time for some payback," he shouted, then shoved the box into me, forcefully, knocking me backward and bouncing me off the door frame.

"Hey, what the hell are you doing?"

He tossed the box to the side and said, "Not so tough now, are you? I'm going to beat you within an inch of your worthless life, you—"

I hit Farrell Finley just as hard as I could. I put all my weight behind the punch, punched right through his chin, snapping his head sideways for the briefest of moments. He stepped back, shook his head as if to clear it, then charged forward, picked me up, and threw me against the wall. "If that's the best you've got, you're in really big trouble," he growled.

"Dev?" Lin called from the kitchen.

"He's busy getting his ass handed to him. You know what's good for you, you'll just stay back there, sweetheart."

I swung at his head and missed. He leaned to the side and smiled, then did the bob and weave thing. I punched at his nose twice and came close, but didn't connect. He pushed my hand down then hit me in the stomach, lifting me off my feet. I felt the wind get knocked out of me. I swung blindly for his chin but hit his shoulder. He just laughed, slapped my face a couple of times, then backhanded me, hard.

"Come on, man, you're fighting like a little girl. At least try to hit me. Not so tough without the gun, are you?"

"Dev, what's going on out…Oh my God," Lin screamed. She stepped around a stack of boxes filled with paints and turpentine in the living room.

"Better back off, sweetheart, there's more than enough of this for two," Farrell said, then delivered two quick punches to my mouth.

"Hey, asshole," Lin yelled. Farrell gave a quick look in her direction just as she stepped forward and sent the palm of her right hand into the tip of his nose. He took a step back, and reflexively grabbed his nose with both hands. Lin spun round like a graceful dancer, came in close, and gave him an elbow right between the eyes. She spun halfway round again and kicked him between the legs, hard, and he half-growled as he dropped to his knees. She spun and sent a fist into the side of his head. Farrell's groan was cut short when she turned sideways and kicked him in the throat. His hands dropped from his bloody nose to his throat as he collapsed onto the floor and curled up into a ball.

She reached down to her ankle and pulled out a small revolver. "I don't know who the hell you are, but you'd better stay right there, or I'll shoot you, so help me God. You hear me?"

Farrell looked up at her with tears running down his cheeks, blood flowing from his nose, and nodded.

"Are you okay, Dev?" she asked.

"Yeah," I said, shaking my hand. It felt like I sprained my wrist when I hit Farrell's shoulder. Shaking my hand not only didn't seem to help, it felt like it was making everything a lot worse. I could feel my lips swelling and tasted blood.

"Here, keep this on dumb shit there. Feel free to shoot him." She handed me her revolver and then moved me back a few feet, so I was out of his grasp. "Let me get my phone. I'll call 911," she said, hurrying back to the kitchen.

"No, don't call them, Lin. We can deal with this here."

Farrell got a wide-eyed look on his face, coughed a couple of times, and half sat up. "Man," he said, then coughed some more and spit a mouthful of blood onto my oak floor. "That is one tough lady."

Twenty-three

Lin took a sip of wine from her glass and said, "I think you're nuts."

"I think it makes perfect sense," Farrell said. He was still on the floor of the front entry, only now he was leaning up against the wall.

"Shut up, idiot," Lin said. "You're lucky I don't finish you off. Dev, that's the dumbest thing I've ever heard."

We were gathered in my front entry, the three of us. I had an ice pack on my lips, Farrell had one on his nose. Rolled tissue was stuffed up both his nostrils. His eyes were partially swollen and growing more purple by the minute. A large bruise ran along the left side of his jawline.

"Dev, forceful entry, assault, we could probably move it up to attempted murder. I've taken pictures of him sitting there on the floor of your front hall. Certainly assaulting a police officer—"

"I didn't know you were a cop. Hey, I got friends who are cops," Farrell rasped.

"I'm not going to tell you again," Lin said.

"Okay, okay, sorry, ma'am."

"Look, the guy was cheating on his wife, and I was gathering evidence."

"And I'm supposed to feel sorry for him?" Lin said.

"I only did it once, honest, and then it didn't even happen." Farrell sounded like he was pleading for his life.

"I'm not going to warn you again," Lin said.

Farrell took one hand off his ice pack and placed it over his mouth.

Lin gave him a disgusted look, then turned to face me. "Do what you want here, darling, but for the record, I think it's a really, really bad idea."

Farrell looked like he was about to say something, then wisely thought better of it and remained quiet.

"He's been under a lot of pressure. I mean, he's got three kids at home, little kids."

"Yeah, right, I get that, so maybe dumb shit here shouldn't have been cheating on his wife, the kids' mom, in the first place. You think?"

"I can't disagree, Lin. All I'm saying is, thanks to you, no real damage was done. Big deal, so I got a fat lip."

"And no brains. He could have killed you, and what about the next time? Or the next person? This sort of thing will just encourage him."

"I don't think so. This has the potential to be so bad. Come on, they'll nail him with three to five years. How's that going to help those kids? It's bad enough the parents will probably be getting a divorce. You pile a prison sentence on top of that. He'll have about zero prospects for a job. That's certainly not going to help with alimony or child support payments."

"Now, there's a good reason to let him off, so he can prey on the rest of society."

"I've got an idea that'll keep him in line, I think."

"Oh, that sounds positive. Okay, it's your place, it's your thick skull. You want to handle things that way, go ahead, and be my guest. But don't come to me when you're in the hospital in traction or worse."

"Thanks, Lin. I knew you'd understand, and I appreciate your help."

"Mmm-mmm," she said, then drained her wine glass and handed it to me.

"Refill?"

"You really are nuts, certifiable. Refill? Are you kidding? I'm getting my ass out of here," she said, then headed back to the kitchen.

"But, but my shoulders? My back rub? I thought you were going to work on helping to relieve my stress?"

"Oh, baby, you've got a lot bigger problem than a little stress," she said, walking back from the kitchen. She had her purse slung over her shoulder. She stopped and blew me a kiss. "Good luck. Here," she said, then reached inside her purse and pulled out a pair of pink, plastic handcuffs. They had fuzzy pink feathers all around them, and the chain links between the two cuffs were all silver and sparkly. "Maybe the two of you can put these to good use. We're sure as hell not going to be using them. Nighty-night, boys," she said and headed out the door.

"Lin? Hey, Lin, wait a minute. Lin? Can we just talk for a minute?" I called from the front porch as she made a bee-line for her car.

"Night, night. Sweet dreams, Dev," she said, without looking back then climbed behind the wheel, started her car, and took off. A car driving past skidded to a stop so he wouldn't hit her, leaned on the horn, then looked over at me and gave me the finger.

"Man, that was close, that guy almost hit her. She didn't even put her lights on," Farrell said. He was standing behind me with the ice pack pressed against his nose, watching Lin's car disappear in the distance. Her headlights were still off.

I looked at him but didn't say anything, then stepped back into the house and closed the door. "Oh shit, I had a great night planned until you showed up."

"Sounds kinda like my entire day. Hey, you got a beer? I could maybe use one right about now."

"A beer? After all this bullshit?"

"Can it hurt? Besides, I was thinking maybe we should talk about what you want from me."

Twenty-four

We were on our second beers, but that was it, only because Demarcus had gone through the rest of the twelve-pack before he left or disappeared or whatever he did, and I wasn't about to share any wine with Farrell. We'd been talking for the better part of an hour. Farrell had a fresh ice pack up against his nose. His throat, where Lin had kicked him, was still bothering him, so thankfully, he was a man of few words, at least for the moment. When he did talk, his voice sounded raspy.

I had hoped to come back into the kitchen and finish what was left of the steaks, but Morton had licked both plates clean. The way my luck seemed to be going at the moment, this was definitely not the time to buy a lottery ticket.

"So, you're going to have to settle things with your wife. I'm under contract to provide her with the photos of you and that Chastity chick, and I intend to do that. However you can work it out with her, that's your business."

"Well, first of all, her real name ain't Chastity."

"Doesn't really matter, Farrell."

"Second, nothing happened."

"Come on, man."

"No, seriously. We got to that Tryst place and she wanted more money. I didn't have it for starters, not to mention a lot of second thoughts bouncing around in my head, so nothing happened. Cost me two hundred bucks to get her for the night and I ended up sleeping in a chair, she slept on the bed, with her clothes on I might add. That don't even count the room charge."

"Farrell, how dumb do I look?"

"I'm not kidding you, dude."

"Not kidding? You arranged a meeting with her more than once. On your home computer I might add. Not the brightest of moves."

"Yeah, I know, but I always chickened out. You can even ask her."

"Look, whatever you decide to do to try and patch things up, you better do it. I'm gonna have to report to the wife within the next few days. You screw up, or try and pull anything on me, I'll have Lin file a police report about tonight. She's got the pictures to prove it, and I'll just tell the cops you ran out the door and got away."

"Hey, you mentioned a way we might work things out, so the cops aren't involved?"

"Yeah, the two guys breaking in here, God, it was just last night. Actually earlier this morning if you want to get technical, although it seems like a week ago. I think they were trying to steal all those paintings." I nodded at the two stacks of paintings next to the backdoor.

Farrell glanced at them and shook his head. "Those things? You gotta be kidding. They actually wanted them? No offense, man, but not exactly a big market for crap like that, is there? Looks like something the kids would do, if I could ever get them off the idiotic video games."

"Well, they broke in here and were about to steal the damn things. That's why they stacked them all up next to the door. Only me fighting the two of them off and chasing them out of here stopped them from taking the things."

Farrell looked at me but didn't comment for a long moment. Then he said, "So, what do you want me to do?"

"Just keep an eye on the place. They're bound to be back. Hell, for all I know, they're scoping the place out as we speak."

"Define keeping an eye on the place."

"Watch it during the night. I can do a lot of work from home, so I'll be here during the day, but the late hours, when I'm asleep, be nice to have someone else here. Someone who can take care of himself."

"Hmmm-mmm, too bad I have to sleep. I got a day job, you know."

"Yeah, with the county, right?"

"Yup. Tell you what, how 'bout I park out in front on the street and crash on your living room couch. If they're checking the place out, they'll know I'm here, and if they try and break in, well, they'll just end up with a lot more than they can handle."

"Yeah, I suppose that could work. We'll start tomorrow night. I won't be sleeping much tonight. In the meantime, you're going to have to come to whatever agreement you can with your wife."

"Jesus, I was so stupid."

I didn't feel the need to respond.

Twenty-five

Farrell left with his ice pack. I didn't envy the task he had in front of him. Idiot.

I set about cleaning the kitchen and loading the dishwasher. I sent Lin a text message a little after ten, then settled down in front of the flat screen in the den, hoping she might have a change of heart and run back over to attend to my needs. The room still had a plaster dust smell, and all of the ceiling that had fallen was still lying on the floor and the coffee table. I just didn't have the energy at the moment to clean it up. I scrolled through the cable channels and Netflix but didn't come across anything that grabbed me, so I turned off the flat screen and began to carry the canvases stacked by the backdoor upstairs to the guest room.

Once in the guest room, I noticed that Demarcus's clothes and suitcase were gone. Between the burglars' assault last night, Colleen Lacy's apparent abduction, Aaron this morning, Lin, and then Farrell Finley screwing up my late-night plans, I hadn't had much time to think about where Demarcus had gone. To tell the truth, he'd become a major pain in the ass, and I was more worried that he might return rather than the fact that he'd left.

It took the better part of an hour, but I got all the splotchy canvasses hauled upstairs. I stacked most of them against a far wall in the guest room. I placed three separate piles on the bed just in case Demarcus showed up and hadn't gotten the message that he'd more than worn out his welcome. I hauled a good portion of the junk from the U-Haul van out of the living room, and up to the guest room then let Morton out into the backyard for a moment.

Once he was back in the house, I double-checked the locks, wedged a dining room chair under the front and backdoor knobs, set the alarm on my cellphone for half-past seven, and settled onto the living room couch beneath a fleece blanket.

The alarm went off the following morning. Morton gave a disgusted look in my direction, then placed his front paws over his ears. I rolled off the couch and headed into the kitchen to put the coffee on, then went upstairs to shower. When I came back downstairs, Morton had stretched out on the couch and pulled the fleece blanket over him.

I went into the kitchen, poured myself a cup of coffee, and thought about calling Aaron LaZelle for any update on Colleen Lacy. I was just about to make the call when the doorbell rang, and I walked out to the front door.

Farrell Finley was standing on the porch. I removed the dining room chair wedged beneath the doorknob, and cautiously pulled the door open.

"Farrell?" Both eyes were black, his nose was swollen, and there was a large dark bruise along his left jawline. He was holding a large suitcase.

"Yeah, hey, umm, sorry about last night. I may have been a little out of line."

"Forget about it. You're dealing with a lot of pressure right now."

"Yeah, no kidding. Ahhh, I'm just on my way to work. Thought the way things were going, it might be a good idea to leave the house early. Mind if I drop this suitcase off here?"

"No, not a problem, I guess that's okay. Things that bad?"

"Let's just say they've been better and leave it at that."

"You're still going to come over here tonight?"

"Yeah, like we agreed. I'll, ahh, camp out on your couch over there if that's okay." He indicated the couch where Morton was stretched out under the fleece blanket.

"Yeah, yeah, sure. Oh, hey, sorry, come on in. You want a coffee?"

"No, I gotta get to the office. No doubt the wife will be calling down there to check on me."

"How'd it go last night?"

"Well, she didn't kill me, and she said we could talk in a couple of days, maybe. So, I guess that's better than nothing. But you could feel the tension in the air when I was making the kids' breakfast."

"Maybe that's about as good as you can expect."

"You hear anything from that woman who kicked my ass last night?"

"Oh, Lin? No, I'd guess she's apparently not all that hard up for male companionship."

"Sorry if I screwed things up for you."

"Amazingly, women always seem to find a reason to head for the hills where I'm concerned."

"Mmm-mmm. Well, look, if I could leave this here." He wheeled his suitcase in next to the couch and stared at Morton for a long moment. "He always sleep like that?"

"Yeah, unless he goes to the office with me, then he sleeps down there."

"Okay, well, I guess I'll see you tonight. I'm gonna try and grab dinner with the kids at home. Then I'll be over maybe eight, nine o'clock once they go down. If that works okay for you."

"That should be fine. I'll be here most of the day. See you tonight, and good luck on the home front."

"Thanks, I'm gonna need it. Ahhh, I just wanted to thank you for not calling the cops last night. I'm sorry I was such a jerk. If it's any consolation, you almost took me out with that first punch."

"I just hope things work out for you two and the kids."

"Thanks. See you tonight," he said, flashed a sad smile, then turned and headed for his pickup.

I watched him drive off, then walked back to the kitchen and called Aaron.

"Please tell me you have something positive to offer," he answered.

"Yeah, good morning to you, too. I was calling about Colleen Lacy. You guys have anything?"

"Have you had any activity?" he asked in response to my question.

"No, nothing. I've got a guy sleeping on my living room couch beginning tonight, just to make it less attractive for those two guys in the event they're thinking of paying me a return visit. No ransom demand or anything like that?"

"What about Demarcus Cantrell? Have you heard anything from him?" Aaron asked, ignoring my second question.

"Not so much as a peep. His clothes are gone, along with a fairly large suitcase. I hauled all those paintings stacked by the backdoor up into my guest room. Piled a number of them on the bed, so if he ever does show up he'll hopefully get the message that he's not welcome."

"I think it might be a good idea if you held onto all those items."

"The paintings?"

"Yeah, as well as the paints, easels, rolls of canvas, books, everything."

"How long do I have to do that?"

"For the time being. We've got this gentleman at some point coming from the Musée d'Orsay in Paris. He may want to look at all that stuff. Just sit on it for a few days, maybe a week, Dev."

"Will you keep me posted on Colleen or Demarcus? I'd like to be in the know. Especially if there's a chance those two idiots who broke in here last night might get a wild hair and return."

"I'll tell you if we get anything I think you should know."

"And this guy from the museum, you don't know when he's going to arrive?"

"No idea, other than in the next few days. It could be today could be in a week. Hell, it could be they decide not to send him, and he never shows. Not really my first priority. How's that head, by the way?"

"It's been worse. I'll live." I didn't see any point in telling him about Lin stopping over, kicking Farrell's fat ass, then throwing her hands up in disgust, storming out of the place, and going home rather than spending the night to take care of my needs.

"You hear anything, anything at all from this Demarcus character, I want to know. Got it? If he contacts you, try and find out where in the hell he is."

"Not a problem. You'll be the first person I call," I said, and Aaron hung up.

I went online and Googled the names Maynor and Pascal, the two names Colleen had told me Demarcus would get late-night calls from. That turned out to be an act of total futility. The first thing Google came up with was Eric Maynor, the basketball player. Next, I checked out the Musée d'Orsay and forgeries. Nothing recent regarding oil paintings by French artist Pierre Auguste Renoir was mentioned. In 2014 a watercolor in possession of the Musée d'Orsay supposedly by artist Auguste Renoir was discovered to be a fake. The watercolor had been forged by a sculptor named Ernest Durig, who claimed to be the last student of Renoir, although other than a photograph of the two together, no proof had ever been presented to prove that particular claim. Durig apparently forged a number of items, claiming they were the work of Renoir. Nothing else was mentioned, which made me wonder about the story Aaron had told me of a fake hanging on the walls of the museum for close to a year.

Just on the odd chance something might happen, I called Colleen Lacy's cellphone but got dumped into her voicemail after four rings. I checked my text messages just in case Lin had responded but knew going in that she hadn't. I called Louie next and got dumped into his voicemail. He called me back a couple of hours later.

"Dev, I think I just missed your call."

"You missed it by a couple of hours, Louie."

"Yeah, probably. What's happening?"

"Just a heads up, I won't be in the office today."

"Oh?"

"Yeah, probably for the next couple of days." I went on to tell him about Colleen Lacy being kidnapped, Demarcus disappearing and the burglars at my place. I left out any reference to Farrell Finley or Lin Nguyen except to say I had someone spending the night here.

"You gonna be okay? I got an open couch at my place."

"Thanks, but no thanks. I'll be fine. Not really in the mood to wander too far, at least not until I get all this art stuff out of the house. I'll tell you, from now on, about all I'm going to be hanging up on the wall are calendars with happy scenes."

"Well, stay in touch. Let me know if I can be of any help."

"Thanks, I'll keep you posted," I said and hung up.

Twenty-six

My phone woke me a little after four that afternoon. I was stretched out on the couch in the living room, Morton was asleep on the floor between a couple of boxes of paint rags and brushes. Some nonsense about redoing a kitchen in an old farmhouse was blathering away on the tube.

"Hello," I groaned, then cleared my throat.

"Gee, sorry, am I waking you?" Aaron said.

"No, just finishing up taking Morton for a walk. Did a couple of miles, but wanted to set a quick pace, don't like leaving the house unattended, at least until I get all this junk out of here," I lied.

"Well, I may have some good news for you. Turns out the French guy from the museum is coming in this afternoon. Some guy named Darcel. As a matter of fact, I'm out at the airport right now to meet him. I was going to take him over to Colleen Lacy's home first, and then I'd like to swing past your place so he can take a look. Does that work for you?"

"Fantastic. Yeah, by all means, bring him over. He can take whatever he wants from here. Once he's seen all this junk, can I get rid of it?"

"I don't see why not. Well, unless you wanted to be a nice guy and hang onto it for your friend."

"Demarcus? The guy who unloaded all this crap here then disappeared without so much as a thank-you or a goodbye? Mmm-mmm, no, I don't think so."

"The plane is listed as having landed. As soon as he clears customs, he'll be out here. Manning's back in passport control now, trying to get him on a little faster track."

"Good luck with that."

Aaron ignored my comment and said, "I'll phone you once we've left Colleen Lacy's place," and then hung up. He phoned back about an hour and a half later.

"Aaron?"

"Hi, Dev. We're just about to head over to your place. Are you home?"

"Yeah, come on over. Want me to put some coffee on or something?"

"Might not be a bad idea. It's close to eleven-thirty at night in Paris, makes for a pretty long day. See you in about fifteen minutes."

"I'll be here."

I made six cups of fresh coffee, then spent the next ten minutes straightening out some of the piles that were scattered around the living room. I had just let Morton out the backdoor when I heard footsteps on the front porch and a moment after that the doorbell.

"Right on time," I said to Aaron as I opened the door. I looked behind him and stared at the attractive dark-haired woman in the short skirt who smiled back at me.

"Dev, this is Darcel Renard. She's with the Musée d'Orsay in Paris. Darcel, this is—"

"Yes, Mr. Devlin Haskell, so very nice to meet you. I understand you've had an interesting last few days," she said, stepping forward and extending her hand. Her accent was almost, but not quite, heavy, and when she took my hand, she smiled and gently rubbed her thumb back and forth over the back of my hand. We were going to get along just fine.

"Please, please, won't you come in, Madame," I said then held the door so she and Aaron could enter. I looked out on the street and noticed that Detective Norris Manning remained in the front seat of the car, which was just fine with me.

"Please, you must call me Darcy, it is what my friends do." She smiled and then gave me a subtle little wink.

"Okay, Darcy, but only if you call me Dev, that's what everyone calls me. Now, I put some coffee on. I didn't know if you were able to catch any sleep on the flight over from Paris. If you'd like some, I can—"

"Yes, it would be just the thing. I'm running on almost empty, I think."

"Come on back to the kitchen then," I said and started toward the back of the house.

"Excuse me. These are the items you had mentioned, Lieutenant?" she said, pointing to the stacks of boxes, easels leaning against the wall and rolls of canvas.

Aaron looked at me.

"That's some of it," I said. "The rest, along with all sorts of canvases and not very good paintings, are piled upstairs in my guest room. Feel free to look at that stuff, and I'll get you that coffee. Do you take it black?"

"Mmm-mmm, yes, that would be best. And, oh!" she said as Morton suddenly came around the corner and thrust his nose under her skirt and between her legs.

"Oh, I'm sorry. You'll have to excuse him. Morton, get the hell over here."

"No, he is nice. Very nice. Morton is the name?"

"That's one of the names I call him."

"Is no harm. Is funny, oui? I like dogs."

"Okay, suit yourself. He'll be your friend for life now. Aaron, you want a coffee?"

"No. Thanks anyway, but I better take a pass. Actually, I wonder if we shouldn't get you checked into your hotel, Darcy. Then I should get back to the office. There's a number of things we're juggling at the moment."

"Any news?" I asked.

Aaron shook his head.

"Oh, I'm sorry. I didn't mean to waste your time. It's just that this is all we've talked about ever since we received word from Interpol, and I would love to take a first look at what Mr. Dev has here. Perhaps I could take a taxi?"

"I tell you what, Aaron, you go ahead and take off. Darcy, if you want to go through these items, please be my guest. I can take her down to the hotel, Aaron, if that's all right with you."

"Would you mind?" he asked her.

"Oh no, not at all, in fact, that would work best, I think. You're sure you don't mind, Mr. Dev?"

"No. Really, it would be my pleasure."

"Okay, great. Thanks for being so understanding, both of you. I'll just head back to the office and let you get to work," Aaron said.

I walked him to the door as Darcy stepped into the living room and gazed over the stacks and piles of Demarcus's crap.

"Dev, thanks for helping. Not so much as a blip on the screen for Colleen Lacy or Demarcus Cantrell. Usually, by now, we've heard something. Unfortunately, that doesn't bode well for either one of them."

"Hopefully, something will turn up. Listen, Aaron, go on back to your office, and I'll deal with this. You need anything, just call."

"Thanks," he said, then hurried out to the car and Manning.

Twenty-seven

Darcy had finished her second cup of coffee a half-hour ago. I'd turned the lights on in the living room a while back so she could see better. She had pulled things out of boxes and was filling a notebook with all sorts of notes recording what she'd found in the boxes. She had me refilling the boxes with things she wanted to review further. The things she didn't need I was stuffing into a trash bag. I already had four of them, trash bags, in the kitchen piled up next to the backdoor.

"He was very clever, your man."

"Demarcus?"

"Yes. These powders, oh no, save that and put it in the box over there, please. Yes, thank you. Yes, your man Demarcus, very clever. With these powders, he has mixed certain paints to formulate colors used in the 1880s and 90s. These days, all paint comes in metal tubes. The tube was invented by a man named John Goffe Rand, in 1841. Before that, artists used glass syringes or pigs' bladders."

"Pigs' bladders? Charming," I said as she handed me a small plastic bag of purple powder and pointed toward a box.

"Yes, I know. Then in 1841, Willim Winsor, of Winsor and Newton invented the screw cap, and the rest is painting history." She smiled at her little joke.

"So, Demarcus was making paints with these powders and mixing them with what? Turpentine?"

"No, linseed oil, actually, duplicating formulas I would suspect. Making the works appear original. Of course, he would still need the proper canvas. Based on what I'm seeing with the paints here, I would have to say he was extremely experienced. Oh my," she yawned.

"Oh, can I get you more coffee? Or maybe you'd like to check into that hotel."

"Mmm-mmm, you know what I would like is a glass of wine. Would that be too much to ask for?"

"No, no, not at all. Coming right up."

"Then, if you would, please point me in the direction of your toilet."

"It's actually upstairs. Just take the stairs, and once you're on the second floor, it's the first door on your left. Just across the hall from the bathroom is my guest room. After the break-in the other night, I carried all the canvases up into that room and stored them in there, along with the rolls of old canvas Demarcus had. Now I'm wondering just how old that stuff really is?"

"Oh, I'd love to see it. You don't mind? I'm sorry. I hope I'm not ruining your evening plans."

"No, not at all. Let me just open a wine bottle, and I'll bring a glass up to you. The stuff is just across the hall from the bathroom."

"Oh, you are so sweet, Mr. Dev," she said, then stood and gave me a kiss on the cheek. She squeezed my forearm as she did so, then stepped back and stared for a moment. "Nice, very nice," she said, then turned and headed for the stairs.

I watched her as she walked out of the living room, across the front entry, and up the staircase. She caught me watching and gave a little wave of her index finger, suggesting 'naughty, naughty,' as she headed up the steps, smiling.

I hurried into the kitchen and opened what I thought was maybe the best bottle of wine Lin had left last night, thinking just maybe it was poetic justice. I half chuckled to myself that less than twenty-four hours later, Darcy and I were going to drink the wine that Lin bought.

I filled two glasses with red wine, pouring the wine through the aerator that Heidi had purchased for me maybe a year ago. It made a funny sound, and everyone said it actually made the wine taste better, although I could never tell the difference. I waited a few minutes just to give Darcy a little privacy before I went upstairs with the wine glasses.

Twenty-eight

When I walked into the guest room, Darcy was down on all fours in the far corner, almost, but not quite, exposing a perfect rear end. She looked like she was sniffing or licking a roll of yellowed canvas, one of a half-dozen I'd stacked in the corner.

"Are you that hungry?" I joked.

She bolted upright then turned and carefully pulled the roll of canvas onto her lap. "This is amazing. If these test positive, and I think they will, you have no idea the value you have sitting here."

"That stuff, it's old and yellow. Who'd want it? You can get the new stuff for a couple of bucks on Amazon, I checked just the other day, and they'll deliver it right to your door."

"Actually, Mr. Dev, this is priceless. Art canvas, easily one hundred, but maybe a hundred and twenty-five years old, that's very rare, and you have six rolls. I've never seen that much. I would say, just looking, your friend Demarcus easily has a few hundred thousand dollars' worth here, possibly a half-million."

"You're kidding, for that shit? Here, you want your wine?" I said and held out a glass of wine in her direction.

"No, please, be careful. Just set the glass over there on the dresser so you, so we don't spill any on this canvas. Could I impose on you to look in my purse in your front room downstairs? There is a small black leather bag in it if you could bring that up to me, the small bag, please."

"Black leather bag in your purse?"

"Yes, if you could bring that to me."

"Be right back." I set the two wine glasses on top of the dresser and hurried out the door. Her purse, a black leather thing with gold buckles and the name "Fendi" embossed on the flap, was lying on the couch with Morton curled around it. Fortunately, it looked like he hadn't chewed the thing. I unbuckled the two leather straps at the bottom and opened it up. The small black leather bag was sitting right on top. I grabbed the bag, then placed the purse on the fireplace mantel so Morton couldn't get to it. There was just the slightest hint of Darcy's perfume lingering around the purse.

"This it?" I asked, holding the leather bag out to her as I walked back into the guest room.

"Yes, yes, perfect. Thank you," she said, taking the bag from my hand. She was still on the floor with the roll of canvas on her lap. She appeared to have unrolled it just an inch or two. She set the leather bag on the floor, opened it, and pulled out a small pair of scissors, what looked like a prescription bottle, and some color chart. She carefully cut a few threads from the edge of the canvas and set them on the chart. Then she unscrewed the bottle and removed an eyedropper. She placed a drop of the liquid over the threads, then returned the dropper to the bottle and screwed it into place. She returned the bottle to the bag, then held the small chart up to examine the threads, nodding as if it all made sense.

"So?"

"So, this was simply an initial field test, but it confirms this canvas to be at least one hundred and twenty-five years old. I can do more testing in the lab when I return home, but this is nothing short of amazing."

"Who would ever hold onto that stuff for over a hundred years?"

"That's part of what makes it so amazing, so rare. No one, actually. On an odd occasion, we may find a small blank canvas, but that's very rare. Constant wars, fires, floods, just life itself, it almost never happens. More often, with forgeries, what we find is someone has created a work over an existing work."

"Someone paints a painting over another painting?"

"Yes, exactly. It's a procedure that was not uncommon with the masters. Certainly the impressionists, were known to reuse a canvas. Remount it with the existing painting reversed so they could paint on a fresh canvas or just paint directly over an existing work. If we have something like that it, of course, immediately raises questions. If the work is legitimate, it will more than likely pass the tests. If, however, it is on a canvas that is authenticated to a particular time period and there is no other painting on it, well, you can see how that might eliminate a number of questions and concerns."

"So, what you're saying is, Demarcus, painting on that old blank canvas, would automatically gain a certain amount of credibility with anyone examining the painting."

"Yes, exactly. And from what I could see at the woman's home—"

"Colleen Lacy."

Darcy nodded. "From what I could see, with the mural on her dining room wall and the three paintings hidden in her closet, this Demarcus had the talent and, now, with everything here, the materials to create uncountable forgeries. He is a very gifted artist in his own right."

"Then why spend his time making fake stuff, or worse, all those splatter things? God, look at them, what an absolute mess. Who in their right mind would ever pay for something like that, let alone hang it up somewhere?"

Darcy glanced at the stack of canvases leaning against the wall, then looked at the three piles on the bed and just shook her head. "That is, as you Americans are so fond of saying, our million-dollar question."

Twenty-nine

Darcy quickly reviewed the stacks of various items I'd carted up to the guest room, then started carefully examining the splattered paintings I'd piled on the bed and against the wall. She wasn't going to just glance or rifle through the stacks. She held a magnifying glass to the first splattered work, closely examined all four sides, the edges of the canvas, the wood frame, and the staples attaching it to the frame. She looked at the back of the canvas, then the front. She did some test on the paint using another eyedropper.

"Are you going to do that on each one of those awful things?"

"I'm sorry, is that too much?"

"Actually, no. I'm fine with that if that's what you want to do to them. Tell you what, I'll leave you to your work. You must be getting hungry?"

"I'm starving, actually."

"Why don't I make some dinner for us? You just keep on working. I'll call you when dinner is ready, probably be about an hour. You get bored, come on down and join me in the kitchen for a glass of wine, but no pressure. You do what you want."

"Oh, you are so kind, Mr. Dev. You're sure it's not a problem for you?"

"You kidding? If your examinations help get this stuff out of my house, you just keep right on working."

"You are too kind. I hope to make it up to you. I promise not to take so long."

"You just take your time. I'll get going on some dinner," I said and headed downstairs. I let Morton out the backdoor, put some music on in the kitchen, then grabbed the steaks I was going to cook for Lin from the refrigerator. I made a salad, wrapped some peppers in foil and placed them on the gas grill outside. About twenty minutes later, I put the steaks on and then called upstairs to Darcy and told her dinner would be ready in ten minutes. When I took everything off the grill and carried the steaks and peppers back into the kitchen, she was already seated at the kitchen counter, in the process of filling her wine glass.

"Oh, I hope it is all right. I was helping myself to some more wine."

"Not to worry. That's one of my rules, I'll get you the first glass, but then you're responsible for any after that."

She smiled, raised her glass, and said, "A la tienne. Oh, sorry, do you speak French?"

"Actually, no. Ummm, I've been thinking of taking lessons, but I guess I just haven't gotten round to it."

She smiled in a way that suggested she didn't believe me, then said, "It means to your health."

I thought about repeating the toast, then figured however I pronounced it would probably sound offensive so just moved on. "I hope you're hungry."

"Starving, I found the food on the airplane disgusting, and so I haven't really eaten since early this morning. Oh, this wine, it is very good. French?"

"No, American, actually, from California. It's a Pinot Noir. One of my favorites, although I usually prefer a beer instead, once in a while, maybe a Jameson whiskey. We'll let these steaks sit for another minute or two. They're rib eyes. I think you'll like them."

"Pig eyes?" She sounded concerned.

"No, rib eyes, like the rib," I said and pointed to my side. "It one of the best cuts of meat."

"Right now, I think I could eat just about anything, even pig eyes, or the airplane food," she said and laughed. She raised her glass and took another sip of wine.

We had a leisurely meal talking about everything and nothing. She told me Paris was her hometown and that she had replaced the man at the museum who had ultimately been responsible for giving approval to the painting that was later determined to be a forgery.

"It was most unfortunate, and under the circumstances, an error that anyone could have made. I was very fond of him. He was the one who hired me to begin with, and I learned quite a bit working at his side. In the end, I found the whole situation of his pending dismissal most uncomfortable. Fortunately, the museum was smart enough to offer him an early retirement and that seemed to quiet things down. To this day, they have never officially acknowledged the fake painting. I still consult with him from time to time, and he always tells me he loves his retirement. But, when I contacted him about the notification from Interpol, you could hear it in his voice. He wanted to be a part of the examination. Unfortunately, there was no way that would ever be permitted. How do you say it? Part of the politics of the business."

We were on our second bottle of wine, enjoying one another's company when the doorbell rang. I glanced at my watch. It was almost nine.

"Who the hell could that be?" I said more to myself than Darcy. "Be back in a minute."

I saw him when I was halfway to the front door. Farrell Finley. I'd completely forgotten. My first thought was to send him on his way, but then with all the rolls of antique canvas upstairs in the guest room worth up to a half-million dollars, I thought maybe having Farrell there wasn't such a bad idea.

"Hey, dude, sorry I'm late, soccer game was tonight, then we stopped for ice cream on the way home. Ended up talking to the wife once I dropped the kids at home," Farrell said, then stepped into the living room.

"How'd it go, talking to the wife?"

"Well, we were in the kitchen, and she didn't stab me with a knife. While we talked, she was reasonably pleasant, so all in all, I guess it went okay."

"Please, make yourself at home, Farrell. I've, ahh, got a friend out in the kitchen. We're just finishing up dinner."

"Oh, sorry, man, hope I'm not cramping your style. Hey, don't take this the wrong way, but it's not that little cop, is it? The one who kicked the shit out of me. I don't want to cross her, and I'd be happy to hide in a corner somewhere if it saved me another beating."

"No, it's not Lin. Actually, it's business. A woman just in from Paris."

"Paris? You do business in Paris?"

"I do business all over," I lied.

"Cool, man. If it's okay I'll just make myself comfortable out here."

"Or, feel free to turn on the tube in the den. Sorry about the plaster mess in there. I meant to clean it up, but some other things just seemed to get in the way over the last couple of days."

"I know how that goes," Farrell said.

"Yeah, I always think I have an open day to just do my shit and then the next thing I know by nine in the morning, there isn't enough time left in the day."

"Good luck, man," he said, then indicated the kitchen with a nod of his head.

"Yeah, thanks, but I don't think it's going to be that kind of a deal, unfortunately."

Farrell looked like he had a comment on the tip of his tongue, then thought better of saying anything. "I'll maybe try and catch something on the boob tube. if that's okay."

"Be my guest, help yourself," I said and hurried back to Darcy in the kitchen.

Thirty

Darcy was on her cellphone, sitting at the kitchen counter, talking French. She smiled at me and nodded as I stepped into the kitchen. I noticed she'd refilled both our wine glasses. I finished the last bits on my plate while standing up, then cleared the counter and loaded the dishwasher. Darcy disconnected her call just as I finished the dishes.

"Oh, my, sometimes I wonder," she said and took a sip of wine.

"Everything okay?"

"Yes, just sometimes, if you're available, even if it's halfway around the world, then no one feels the need to make a simple decision. Nothing that couldn't have been handled without me, but even three years after the forgery was discovered, we are all still walking on the eggs as you say."

"Walking on eggshells?"

"Yes, the shells, that's what I meant to say. Mmmmmm, I have to say your wine is excellent."

I couldn't remember if Lin or Heidi had brought this particular bottle. Certainly, one of them had, not that it mattered at this point. "Yeah, like I said before, one of

Art Hound • 155

my favorites. I order special direct from the winery," I said and took a sip.

"Oh, really?"

"Oh, yeah. I travel out to the west coast wine country a number of times a year. Buying trips," I lied, trying to sound classy.

"I never would have guessed," she said, sounding like she maybe knew more than she was letting on.

"Now that I think about it, I think I'd laid in a case or two from someplace that was going out of business, picked the stuff up for something like a third of the original price. My guests always seem to like it, so the stuff has served me well."

We chatted back and forth for another hour. It was a little after ten and halfway through another bottle of wine before I realized what time it was. "Oh, man, I've been asleep at the switch, here. We haven't checked you into the hotel yet."

"Oh, I completely forgot. I wonder, umm, would it be too much to ask if I could impose. I don't wish to cause you a problem."

"Oh, you wouldn't be imposing, believe me," I said, then cursed that jackass Demarcus, not for the first time today. "The only problem is, my guest room is crammed full of splattered paintings, rolls of canvas, and all that other stuff. I would gladly sleep on the couch, but I've got Farrell Finley staying here for some added protection after that break-in the other night. So I can't really sleep there, and—"

"I don't wish to impose, but maybe you should not worry about these little things. Have some more wine and see how things come to work themselves out," she said, then smiled, raised her eyebrows, and took another sip of wine.

"You mean—"

"I mean, you should not worry yourself. Let's just enjoy the night and see what happens."

We had another glass of wine, and then Darcy said, "Shall we go up the stairs? I would like to see your room."

I grabbed the half-finished bottle of wine, our third, and led the way. Cheers and jeers were coming from the den, and I poked my head in as we went down the hallway. Farrell was seated in my recliner, amidst all the pieces of plaster ceiling still scattered across the floor and the coffee table. He was watching MMA News on the Ultimate Fight Club channel. Two bloody guys, each with about a hundred grand worth of tattoos, were busy battling it out, trading punches and kicks.

"Hey, Farrell, why don't you hang onto this house key? I'm not sure what my schedule is going to be tomorrow. Just let yourself in if I'm not around. Everything's locked up. We're heading upstairs. Sleep tight."

He reached over and took the house key, then gave me the thumbs up. "I'm out of here about seven tomorrow morning, Dev, so I'll . . . Cheri?" he said, looking over my shoulder at Darcy standing behind me. He suddenly had a wide-eyed, shocked look on his face.

"What?"

"Cherri?"

"No, I'm sorry, but you are mistaken, I think. You must be thinking of someone else."

"You're not Cherri?"

"I'm Darcy."

"Darcy?" he said and leaned forward in the chair for a closer look.

"Darcy is over from Paris, helping me and, well, the cops on an ongoing case. Kind of complicated."

"Yes, I'm from Paris," Darcy said. Her accent seemed to have grown heavier.

"Oh, sorry, you just looked like someone I met once. But I guess not. Huh, amazing. You could be her twin."

"I have never been here in your Minnesota before. It is very nice. Mr. Dev, I see you upstairs, I want to take one more quick look at the paintings."

"I'm right behind you, Darcy. See you, Farrell."

"Thanks again, Dev," he said, then flashed me the 'Okay' sign with his right hand.

Darcy grabbed a small suitcase from the front entry, and I followed her up the stairs, enjoying the view from maybe five feet behind. She half paused at the door to the guest room, then turned and looked at me. "Your room?"

"Is just a little further down the hall," I said, taking the lead. Darcy followed close behind, rubbing her hand back and forth across my shoulder. I opened the door and stepped into my bedroom, then closed the door behind her. "You sure you're okay with this?"

"More than okay, Mr. Dev. It's what I've wanted since I first arrived. Oh, I love the bed," she said, setting the suitcase down, then sitting on the edge of my bed and rubbing her hand across the sheets. She ran her hand suggestively up and down one of the carved bedposts at the foot of the bed, then took another sip of wine and stuck her leg out.

I must have given her a funny look.

"My shoe, Mr. Dev, I'm not going to wear it in bed. In fact, I don't plan on wearing anything, except maybe a smile."

She sipped her wine while I pulled her shoes off, then massaged her feet. She slid off the bed, drained her glass of wine, and handed me the empty. I set the empty on the top of the dresser, quickly finished my glass, and when I turned round, she had her back to me and was in the process of unbuttoning her blouse.

"Mmm, Mr. Dev, rub my shoulders for just a little moment, please. Oh, yes, that is wonderful, wonderful. I think you may have done this once or twice before. Yes, yes, oh perfect, that is so good. So good."

She suddenly dropped her skirt to the floor, kicked it over to the side, and then moved her arms in one fluid motion, and her blouse dropped to the floor. I glanced down at the hint of a small red thong just below the tattoo at the base of her spine. The tattoo was about the size of a dinner plate and looked familiar.

"Is, is that the logo for the Montreal Canadiens? The hockey team?"

"Oh yes, a cousin, umm, a distant cousin, very distant, once played for them and, well, too much wine the last time they won, and we celebrated, in Paris."

"The guy won the Stanley Cup?"

"Yes, that is it, this cup you speak of, the cup of Stanley," she said. She reached behind her back, undid her bra, and then turned to face me.

I suddenly refocused and any thoughts of the Montreal Canadiens and the Stanley Cup quickly disappeared.

Thirty-one

Morton barking outside the bedroom in the hallway woke me the following morning. I gradually opened my eyes and eventually focused on the digital clock on my dresser. It was close to ten. Bright slits of sunlight were cutting into the room along the edges of the window shades.

I quietly groaned as I slid out of bed, pulled on my boxers, and glanced back at Darcy in the bed. She was snoring softly with the very corner of the bed sheet strategically draped over her midsection. With all the wine we'd consumed, I had a headache and a hazy memory at best of the late-night activities. I did seem to recall we'd gone on for a couple of hours or was it that we'd just had a few rematches over the course of the early morning hours? I couldn't really recall.

I opened the door just as Morton barked again.

"Hey, shut up, man, she's still sleeping," I said in a harsh whisper.

Morton bounded past me and ran to the far side of the bed. He jumped back and forth, grabbed Darcy's red thong off the floor, shot past me, and down the stairs.

Darcy pulled my pillow over her head, never waking up, then rolled over on her side. I studied the tattoo for a long moment, decided it had to be one of, if not *the*, best hockey tattoo I'd ever seen, then took off after Morton.

I closed the bedroom door behind me and half-whispered, "Morton, damn it, bring that back here. Morton!" Not that it did any good.

I caught up to him at the kitchen door, tried to pull the thong from his mouth, and heard it tear roughly in half. "Oh, great, now look what you did, idiot," I said and opened the backdoor. He bounded into the backyard, looking like he could not have cared less. He ran around the backyard twice, then faced me and squatted, all the while holding what was left of Darcy's thong in his mouth. I closed the door, made a pot of coffee, then set the kitchen counter for breakfast for two.

I was on my third cup of coffee and still moving very slowly when I heard some noise upstairs. Fifteen minutes later, Darcy appeared in the kitchen wearing a black t-shirt of mine from The Spot bar. She placed both hands on her temples, raising the t-shirt just enough for a quick view as she slowly shook her head back and forth.

"Oh, my head. I may never drink wine again. How did I end up in your bed?" she said, but then smiled. "Thank you. A wonderful night, very wonderful."

"Thank you. Very nice, I think. I'm not sure I remember everything."

"Your head?"

"It's taking it's time coming around. Would you like a cup of coffee?"

"Oh, yes, please." I poured a mug, handed it to her, and she said, "Can we sit in your living room?"

"Yeah, I suppose, if you want. All those boxes are piled in there, the easels, and stuff."

"If we could, it will help me think and get organized."

"Sure, come on. I'll just go upstairs and put some clothes on and—"

"Oh, no, don't, please. I like this. It is okay with you?"

"Yeah, sure, come on," I said and headed out to the living room.

Fortunately, there wasn't so much as a trace of Farrell Finley in the living room, well, except for his suitcase standing up against the wall. The two chairs on either side of the fireplace were covered with boxes of Demarcus's odds and ends and a couple of canvas drop cloths. We sat down on the couch since it was the only place to sit. We were seated close together, not quite touching. Darcy turned and faced me, softly rubbing my shoulder and neck. Occasionally she glanced out the front window at the passing traffic.

After a few minutes, she took a sip of coffee, gave a satisfied little gasp, and gently lowered her hand to my leg, running it back and forth over my thigh. "Can I just tell you, Mr—" A strange sound suddenly emanated from her purse lying on the fireplace mantel. "Oh, a phone call. Mmm-mmm, probably more silliness from the museum, checking up on me."

She set her coffee mug on the floor, then hurried over to her purse, pulled her phone out, and answered without looking to see who was calling.

"Oui? Oh yes, good morning, Lieutenant," she said and raised her eyebrows in my direction.

Aaron LaZelle, calling her.

"Oh, no, thank you, but that won't be necessary. I've so much, how do you say, to study, to do? Yes, that is the word, analyze. I have so much of this analyze to do that I took a taxi very early, and I'm at Mr. Dev's home now. I will be doing the analyze all day." She smiled at me and raised her eyebrows suggestively.

"Oh, no, thank you, but that will not be necessary. Mr. Dev has been wonderful, most satisfying. Yes, yes, I will. I'm not sure, but we are moving in that direction. The early tests I've performed on the materials certainly point to that, and the little bit of his work I've been able to examine would indicate the same, but it is still too early to say for sure. Yes, I will, thank you. No, it is not a problem at all. Yes, thank you. And have you heard from him? Mr. Demarcus? Or the woman, Claudia Lacy? Oh, yes, sorry, Colleen. Mmm-mmm, I see. Well then, I'll get back to work. Thank you for the phone call. Yes, you also."

"Everything, okay?"

"More than okay. Now it will be wonderful," she said, smiling as she sat down next to me. "They have no news of your friend, this Demarcus person. And—"

"'Friend' has become too strong a term for that freeloader."

"I fear he is much more than that."

"And I take it nothing on Colleen Lacy."

"Not a word." She smiled.

"I suppose you'd like to get back to work."

"Maybe in a moment. Could I talk you into one more cup of coffee?"

"Yeah sure, no problem," I said. I picked her mug up off the floor and headed out into the kitchen. I glanced out one of the kitchen windows. Morton was lying in the sun, in the middle of the backyard, chewing what was left of Darcy's red thong. I just shook my head and filled our coffee mugs, then headed back out to the living room.

Darcy was standing in front of the fireplace, on her phone, speaking in French. She smiled, took the coffee mug from me, and gave me a kiss on the cheek, then quickly nibbled my ear, and kissed me on the lower neck.

I sat back down on the couch and waited until she was off the phone.

"Oh, sorry, more silliness, but it is sorted now."

"So, is your head getting any better?"

"You know what would help, I think?"

"What? You name it. I've got some aspirin upstairs. I usually don't take them, but if you . . ."

She set her mug on the floor, then suddenly knelt down in front of me, pulled The Spot bar t-shirt over her head, and tossed it off to the side.

"Yeah, or this might work," I said.

"Mr. Dev, you just sit back, and we'll both enjoy."

Thirty-two

I didn't hear them come in, but then again, I was otherwise focused. Suddenly, they were standing in the entry to the living room, two of them wearing extremely broad smiles.

"I'm sorry, are we interrupting?"

"Jesus Christ," I shouted and attempted to get to my feet. The fat man took a step toward me. I made a move to the side, but half tripped on my boxers wrapped around my ankles. He gave half a grunt and knocked me back onto the couch by thrusting his massive stomach into me.

Naked Darcy sat back on the floor, smiled, and said something to them in French, and the fat man replied.

They were the two guys who'd broken in the other night. They had to be. Not that I could actually recognize them. Yeah, they were dressed in black, top to bottom, and I don't think I'd ever seen the taller, thinner of the two. He was probably the one who'd given me the karate chop to the back of my neck. But even without the balaclava, the fat man looked the same, or at least his figure did.

He was maybe my height, with a beer belly that hung over his belt. He was partially bald, with neatly trimmed hair that looked like it was the product of a cheap, home dye job. His nose was large, his face had somewhat swarthy skin, and he had dark brown eyes. He sported a neatly-trimmed goatee with flecks of grey. He appeared to be older than sixty, but he could have been mid-fifties and just a product of hard living.

His partner was over six feet tall, lean, but lean in a way that suggested good physical conditioning rather than just being scrawny, perhaps a runner. He had a full head of dark hair, neatly groomed, with a sharp part. Like the fat man, he had dark-brown eyes, but pale skin, maybe due to inside employment as opposed to someone who worked outdoors. He had a large Adam's apple that bobbed a few times as he positioned himself just a foot or two away from me. His face wore a dark, heavy stubble that looked like it hadn't been shaved for the past couple of days.

The fat man said something to Darcy in French and extended his hand.

"Leave her the hell alone," I said and attempted to get to my feet. The lean guy pushed me back down and raised an index finger as if in a warning.

Darcy turned and smiled at me. "It is okay, Dev. Relax. They're friends, very good friends," she said. I noticed that her accent had suddenly seemed to disappear. She turned and said something to the fat man in French, grabbed the discarded t-shirt from off the floor, gave

Fatty a kiss on the cheek, and then headed upstairs with the t-shirt in her hand.

We all stared as she headed up the stairs until she was out of sight, then they refocused their attention on me. They looked at the shocked expression I must have had on my face and chuckled.

I sat quietly on the couch for a few minutes, then said, "Hey, either of you guys speak-a the English?"

"Perhaps a modest amount," Fatty said.

"Mind if I pull my boxers up?" I said, and half lifted my ankles.

"I think it would be a very good idea, much appreciated."

Darcy came back down the stairs a few minutes later wearing a pair of blue jeans and a cream-colored blouse. She said something to Fatty in French, he responded, they went back and forth like that for a minute or two, apparently discussing something. Then Fatty gave the lean guy a nod and walked out the front door. He returned a minute later carrying a large roll of duct tape and handed it to the lean guy, who proceeded to tape my ankles and my wrists.

He asked Fatty something in French, and then Fatty said to me, "We will leave you for the moment on the couch. Feel free to recline. If you make a sound, we will strike you and then tape your mouth. Please nod if you understand and do not make a comment."

I nodded yes, then was about to say something.

Fatty raised his hand and said, "I warn you, so much as one word, and we will tape your mouth. You will find the experience most unsatisfactory. Simply nod if you understand."

I nodded.

The lean guy seemed to effortlessly lift two boxes off one of the chairs by the fireplace. I happened to remember that the boxes were filled with coffee table art books and weighed about fifty pounds each. He stacked the boxes of books on the floor, wiggled an index finger at me, then helped me to my feet. He turned me around, then guided me into the chair he'd just cleared. Once seated, he wrapped duct tape around my chest and the chair a good half-dozen times, securing me in place, then he did the same thing to my legs. Not so tight that it was uncomfortable, but it seemed pretty clear to me I wasn't going to be leaving anytime soon.

Fatty stepped over and pulled on the duct tape, then smiled, nodded, and Darcy led them upstairs. They were back down, Fatty and the lean guy, a few minutes later. Darcy remained upstairs.

The two guys began hauling some boxes out of the living room and stacking them near the front door. As near as I could remember, the boxes were the ones Darcy had me place the various bags of pigment and some antique brushes in.

She appeared some minutes later carrying one of the rolls of blank, antique canvas down the stairs and leaning it next to the boxes by the front door. She made about three or four trips with the rolls of canvas, then said something to Fatty and headed for the kitchen. Fatty and his pal started hauling paint-splattered canvases down from the guest room and leaning them against the wall in the front entry. They had about a dozen canvases lined up when Darcy walked out from the kitchen carrying two plates with sandwiches and bottles of Summit beer.

Both guys said something in French, then sat down on the couch and started in on the sandwiches.

Darcy joined them a moment later with a sandwich and a glass of water. She sat on the floor with her back against the door frame. "Oh, my head, Dev, quite the night. I must have enjoyed myself. I can't remember a thing," she said, then smiled and took a large bite from her sandwich. She said something to the two guys in French and then inclined her head in my direction. They both glanced over at me and laughed.

At some point, I heard my cellphone ring from out in the kitchen, and Darcy hurried out to grab it. She carried the cell back out to the living room. The ring grew louder as she approached, and she showed the phone to Fatty and said something in French.

He nodded, said something back, stuffed the remainder of his sandwich in his mouth, and rose off the couch. All three of them suddenly seemed to pick up their pace, quickly stacking things by the front door.

They left their plates on the floor, the empty beer bottles on a window sill, and proceeded to carry the stacked items out the door. I guessed they had a car or a truck out there, although from where they'd positioned the chair, I couldn't see out the window. In short order, Darcy hurried up the stairs, then came back down carrying her small suitcase. She handed the suitcase to the lean guy, who headed out the door. A moment later, I heard an engine start-up. It sounded heavy-duty, like a truck as opposed to some car.

Darcy and Fatty conversed in French, and Fatty stepped over to me, pulled off a six-inch length of duct tape, and tore it from the roll.

"Aw, come on, I did just what you folks wanted. Don't be an ass—"

He wrapped the duct tape across my mouth, cutting me off in mid-sentence. He tossed the roll on the floor, patted me on the head, said, "Je vous remercie," and headed out the front door.

Darcy watched him for a long moment, then turned and headed down the hallway to the kitchen. She was back a half-minute later, carrying two bottles of Pinot Noir.

"I know you won't mind, Dev. We'll be celebrating," she said, raising both bottles shoulder height just in case I'd missed the fact she was taking them. She set the bottles on the floor, giggled, then pulled my boxers down below my knees, kissed me on both cheeks, and smiled. She stepped back, took her cellphone out, snapped a picture, then said, "I don't care what all the other girls say, I thought you were very good. Au revoir mon amour." She grabbed the wine bottles off the floor, chuckling, paused at the front door for a final look, then set the lock and laughed as she pulled the door closed behind her.

I wanted to scream and would have except for the fact that my mouth was covered with duct tape. I wiggled, strained, tried to force my way loose, and in the end, wound up sweating and panting through my nose, all the effort not doing a thing to loosen the duct tape.

My cellphone, still on the fireplace mantel, rang a number of times over the course of the afternoon, but after the first call, it only gave three or four rings then stopped. I figured that was more a function of the call getting dumped into my voice mail rather than anyone hanging up.

At one point, about mid-afternoon, someone rang the doorbell, pounded on the front door, and then, a few minutes later, pounded on the backdoor. I tried to make noise and cause the chair to jump and thump, but I couldn't get the heavy chair off the floor. Whoever it was apparently didn't hear me and eventually went away.

Thirty-three

It was almost dark outside, so it had to be sometime after eight when there was a knock on the front door. After another knock I could hear a key being inserted into the front door, and a second later, the lock clicked as the door opened.

"Dev? Dev, you home?" Farrell Finley called.

I tried to make some noise, but he apparently didn't hear me. He flicked on the light in the entryway, gave off a tired sounding groan, then made his way back to the kitchen, turning on lights as he went. I remained in the dark, duct-taped to the chair in the living room. I thought I heard the refrigerator door open and close, then a bottle being opened a moment later. I could hear Farrell slowly heading back from the kitchen. Then all was quiet for a long moment before I heard the sound of the flat screen playing in the den. It sounded like a baseball game.

Farrell appeared in the entrance to the living room, maybe fifteen minutes later. As he stepped in, he kicked the plate that Darcy had left on the floor and growled, "What the hell?"

He flicked on the light and stared at the plate now in the middle of the floor with a bread crust lying a few inches beyond. "What stupid son of a bitch?"

His eyes seemed to run across the floor, past the bread crust, to me, duct-taped to the chair, with tape across my mouth, and my boxers pulled down below my knees.

He stared, took a couple of long swallows from his beer bottle as his eyes grew wide. "Oh, dude, man, that is really fucked up."

I moaned and grunted, shifting my head from side to side, and attempted to kick my legs, failing miserably.

Farrell took another long sip, stared at me, then set his beer bottle on the fireplace mantel and cautiously approached. He studied me for a moment, then said, "This is liable to hurt, man."

He worked the end of his thumb under a corner of the duct tape. "Hang on, Dev," He said, then suddenly ripped the duct tape from my mouth.

I gave a loud, short scream, as the tape peeled off a layer of my lips. "Arghh. Oh, God, Jesus Christ. Get me out of this damn chair. I've been here since this morning. God."

"That Cherri bitch, right? I knew it, she—"

"Farrell, get me out of this chair. Get a knife and cut this damn tape."

"Hang on, man," he said, then grabbed the beer bottle off the mantel, took a swig, and reached into his pants pocket.

"Farrell, damn it."

"Dude, relax, stay cool. I'm on it," he said and pulled out his car keys. He opened a small jackknife on his key ring, bent down, and cut the duct tape on either side of my legs. He cut the tape from around my ankles, then my wrists and finally the tape on either side of my chest.

"Oh, man, thank God," I gasped as I stood up from the chair.

"Maybe do us both a favor and pull them boxers back up," he said, turning his head away from me.

I pulled my boxers up, then ripped off the duct tape that was still attached to my legs and ankles. I hurried upstairs, calling as I ran, "Back in a minute." I pulled the duct tape from my chest, tossed it over the banister, then raced into the bathroom.

After what seemed like fifteen minutes of relief, I went into my bedroom. I was thinking there was still just a hint of Darcy's perfume lingering in my bed, but I didn't want to take the time to check it out. I pulled on some jeans, slipped into the Spot Bar t-shirt Darcy had worn, now laying on the edge of the bed and went back downstairs. Farrell was still standing by the fireplace mantel, in the process of draining his beer.

"Hey, look, man, no need to explain. I mean, whatever kink you're into is okay with me. I happen to think it's more than a little weird, but that's just me. The whole bondage deal just doesn't happen to be my thing."

"Farrell, they were here. The guys who broke in the other night. It was all a setup. I don't think that Darcy chick was from Paris," I said, grabbing my phone from the fireplace mantel. I checked my phone log, five calls from Aaron.

"That broad, who said she was from Paris? I knew it was Cherri when I saw her last night. You mean she was part of breaking in? God, I just knew that was her, even sounded like her, the little bit she said. Oh, man, I knew it. What'd you say her name was again?"

"She told me, 'Darcy,' but that had to be a lie. You called her Cherri?"

"Yeah, another one of my failed attempts at getting laid. Cost me a hundred bucks for about five minutes of conversation. She told me she was from over in Montreal. She was a big fan of—"

"Of the Canadiens, right? I knew it. How could I be so stupid? She had a big Montreal Canadiens logo tattooed—"

"Yeah, right above her ass, right? I saw it, but that's as close as I got to scoring. Hey, get it?" he laughed. "A hockey team and I said, that's as close as I got to score—"

I gave him a look that shut him up, then pressed the screen to return Aaron's call.

"She told me she had a distant cousin who played for the Canadiens, and I was stupid enough to believe her. Said she got that tattoo when they won the Stanley Cup. That would have been back in 1995."

"Sorry, dude, but it was all the way back to ninety-three, ancient history."

"God, I was so stupid. She would have been about nine years old. A tattoo, I don't think—"

"You were thinking with the wrong head again, dude."

"I just can't believe . . . Aaron," I half-screamed as he answered.

"Hey, where the hell have you guys been? You weren't answering your phone. Darcy isn't answering. I sent someone over, but you were gone, then I find out you never brought her down to her hotel. I got a phone call from—"

"Aaron, listen, we've been set up. She was here with the guys who broke in the other night. They tied me up, took off with a bunch of Demarcus' stuff, and—"

"What?"

Thirty-four

Farrell was on his fourth beer, sitting at the kitchen counter with Aaron and me. Aaron was asking questions and taking notes. Manning was standing on the far side of Farrell, smiling, almost laughing, sipping coffee from my Las Vegas Bellagio mug and obviously enjoying himself. He seemed to be the only one doing so.

"You didn't look at any identification?"

"Aaron, the only reason she was here in the first place is because you brought her here. You're the one who introduced me to her. Identification? She has a tattoo that says Montreal Canadiens—"

"Right above her ass. She's got a great ass," Farrell said.

"Manning," I said. "You think this is funny? You're the one who pulled her out of the line from passport control when she was going to clear customs, so technically it's really your fault that she—"

"Now hold on there a minute, Haskell. I did not get her out of customs," he said and set down the Las Vegas coffee mug, shaking his head.

"Actually, I did," Aaron said. "I don't believe it. She called me on the phone, told me she'd transferred flights in JFK, cleared customs out there, and was just heading down to grab her suitcase. I met her at carousel five or six. I forget which one, and then I called Detective Manning to join us so we could get moving. God, they probably dropped her off at the airport, and she just walked into baggage claim and called me. How stupid," he said and slapped his forehead. "Christ, they've been two steps ahead of us the whole time."

"She had baggage?" I said.

"To tell you the truth, no, I mean, not much. She just had a small grey suitcase. I said something, and she told me it was going to be a quick trip. I didn't think to question it. We were at the airport, so it seemed to make sense. Now looking back . . ."

"And you recognized her last night?" Manning asked Farrell.

Farrell looked at me to see if it was safe to answer. "Go ahead. They just want information."

"Yeah, I had a dealing with her a few months ago. I, umm, maybe lined up a meeting with her from a website. Cost me a hundred bucks, and I chickened out at the end. I thought she looked familiar last night. When I met her, back a few months ago, she was using the name, Cherri. What'd you say she called herself last night?"

Both Aaron and I said, "Darcy," at the same time.

"Yeah, and that's who Dev said she was last night, that's the name she used. Course when I got here tonight, and he mentioned the tattoo above her ass, I—"

"Montreal Canadiens," I said and shook my head, still having trouble believing I could ever be so stupid.

"Yeah, not too many chicks walking around with one of those. Thing's at least this big," Farrell said and held his hands up.

"Bigger," I said. "Half again as large, about the size of a dinner plate. God."

"You two would be the authority," Manning laughed out loud. "Oh, sorry, but it's all just too perfect." He cleared his throat a couple of times and seemed to grow serious. "They were talking French?"

I nodded.

"You understand any of it?"

"No, I don't speak the language. I did notice her accent more or less disappeared once those two guys showed up. She seemed to be fluent in both English and French, but nothing like the accent we heard yesterday," I said to Aaron.

"That and the tattoo would seem to suggest Canada, certainly Quebec if not Montreal. And you've no idea what they were driving?"

"Like I said, it just sounded like a heavy motor, I'm guessing a truck, but I've no way to be sure."

"Color?"

"I just got finished telling you I didn't see the vehicle. Hey, for all I know it could have been a motorcycle.

I don't know, by the time they started the engine I was duct-taped to the damn chair."

A guy in an ugly green and red plaid sport coat suddenly walked into the kitchen. He was wearing a pair of blue latex gloves, which he proceeded to pull off as he approached. "We're pretty much finished, Lieutenant. Not a lot to go on. Got a couple of long hairs off the pillows from the kingsized bed in the bedroom. That, ahh, thong from the backyard is virtually worthless. We bagged what was left of it, but it looks like the dog enjoyed any telltale traces." He tried to keep a straight face then burst into a wide grin.

Manning shook his head and growled, "Jesus Christ, nice work, Haskell."

"Thanks, Gary," Aaron said and continued to stare at the kitchen counter, slowly shaking his head.

"All the surfaces we checked seemed to have been wiped down. We dusted, just in case, but I'll be surprised if anything turns up. They're thinking there might be a tire tread alongside the driveway. We checked, it doesn't match Mr. Haskell's car or Mr. Finley's F150. We've poured a cast, and we'll go through the analyzation process once we get it over to the BCA. Anything else any of you can think of?"

I figured the tire tread was from Manning's jerk move the other day. Maybe if they traced it back to him, he'd get in trouble so I didn't say anything. "You got the beer bottles, the water glass, and the plates?" I said.

"Yeah. Someone took the time to wipe them down. As far as prints go, we couldn't come up with anything."

"Okay, thanks again, Gary. Anything pops up, anything at all, you let me know."

"Will do, LT, gentlemen," he said, then headed back out of the kitchen.

"You got a laptop here?" Aaron said to me.

"Yeah."

"Get it. Farrell, I want you to log on to that escort site and see if you can find an image of that woman."

"Cherri?"

"Yeah, or whatever she's calling herself now. Bring that laptop in here, Dev."

Farrell logged on to my computer a minute or two later, then onto the escort site, Night Kandy. He signed onto the site using the name 'Studmuffin1'.

"You guys sure I'm not going to get in trouble for this?" Farrell said, he sounded genuinely worried.

"Farrell, you're aiding us in an ongoing investigation, a kidnapping investigation, no less. We find something here, we just might give you a medal," Aaron said.

Farrell looked at Aaron for a long moment, still not seeming too sure.

"Go ahead. You won't get in any trouble. You're not doing anything wrong. You're trying to help us, it's okay."

Farrell shrugged and typed the name Cherri in the search area on the upper right-hand corner of the screen.

The screen displayed a spinning circular symbol suggesting it was searching, and then a number of names appeared, Cherry, Cheryl, Cheryll, Kerry, Kari, and Kara, but nothing with Cherri.

"She must have taken it down, her site," Farrell said.

"How long ago were you on it?" Manning asked.

"At least three, maybe four months ago. It's, umm, not all that unusual that a site disappears. I'm guessing they maybe get out of the business, leave town or change the name they're working under. Sorry."

Aaron made note of the site name, and the URL then said, "Okay, well, thanks for trying. You going to be okay?" he asked me.

"What's to worry about? They've apparently already left with everything they wanted. Thanks, but I'm fine."

"I'll be in touch tomorrow," Aaron said and headed toward the door. He stopped, then turned toward us. "Mr. Finley, thank you for your help. We'll be in touch. Goodnight, gentlemen," he said and headed out of the kitchen. I followed behind him, but he just gave me a quick nod and went out the door. Manning was already behind the wheel of the car, waiting for Aaron.

I watched them pull away from the curb and disappear around a distant corner. I stood there thinking for a long moment, then closed and locked the door. Farrell was in the kitchen, still sitting at the computer. He'd managed to open another beer for himself.

"Anything?" I asked.

"No, I've tried three separate times and come up with the same response, a bunch of names, but not the one we're looking for."

"I'm guessing Aaron'll have some computer genius get on it. Maybe they'll be able to shake some answers loose."

"Yeah, that's great if the site is local. But it almost certainly isn't. Be lucky if it's even hosted in the States. Chances are it's coming from somewhere like Latvia or Uzbekistan or someplace if they can even find out."

"Look someone else up for me, will you, Farrell?"

"Who?"

"Chastity."

"What? Come on, man, I'm the one who got you out of that chair. Those bastards just left you there all taped up. You could have starved to death, and now you want to add another problem to my life?"

"Hardly. Just see if you can get her site up. It's a long shot, but it just might work."

Thirty-five

It took some doing and another beer, but Farrell eventually brought Chastity's site up. She looked a lot less harsh than she had in person the other morning over in Wisconsin. I guessed the result of a lot of applied Photoshop skills.

"There she is," Farrell said and took a very long pull on his beer bottle. "I don't know what the hell I was thinking."

I pulled my laptop over in front of me and started clicking keys.

"What are you doing?"

"I'm trying to line up a date tonight if she's not already booked. How fast does she respond?"

"Chastity? It depends. Sometimes right away, other times, it was a full day. I'm not following what you're trying to do."

"The cops got about a one percent chance of finding Darcy or Cherri or whatever name she's using now, and you hit the nail on the head. This site is probably hosted outside the US, and they won't even bother to respond to a request for information. But even if it's hosted outside the country, all these women are local. Maybe they've run into one another, know where they shop or drink, or God forbid, live."

"You think?"

"If you got a better idea, I'm all ears."

"Actually, no, I don't. Hey, umm, don't mention my name, okay?"

"Not a problem. Besides, I want to be on her good side. If memory serves, didn't you leave her stranded over in Wisconsin?"

Farrell shook his head, then finished his beer. He got off his kitchen stool, opened the refrigerator, and grabbed another beer.

The sound of him opening the bottle seemed to trigger something in me, and I said, "Hey, grab me one of those, will you?"

He took a long swallow, then opened the door and bent over, scanning the contents. He reached in and moved some items around, then stood up and said, "Sorry, dude, looks like you're out. You want a sip?" he said and held his bottle out to me.

"You're kidding. I'm out? God, thanks, but no thanks. I can live without it. Okay, I'm telling her I want to get together, tonight if possible, if she can't make it tonight then tomorrow. I guess now we just sit back, wait and see if she responds."

I made us both a couple of bacon, lettuce, and tomato sandwiches, ate an apple, had a dish of ice cream, then moved into the den and watched Jimmy Kimmel

Live, checking my laptop maybe two dozen times during the course of the show. Nothing.

By the time Jimmy Kimmel signed off, I had pretty much given up. "That's it, man, I'm hitting the sack," I said.

Farrell had pulled in a chair from the dining room since the couch in the den was still covered with chunks of plaster and a lot of dust. "Yeah," he said. "Kind of turned into a late night. You think those two cops will get back in touch with me?"

"Only if they need your help. If you're worried about them coming after you because you knew how to log onto that escort site and knew the name of that woman, don't sweat it. You didn't do anything against the law and in fact you were aiding in an investigation that has been going nowhere. Believe me, they're frustrated, and they got nothing, and I mean nothing, to go on."

"Okay, if you say so. You know, you might want to get this place cleaned up. It'd be a pretty nice room if you got all this plaster shit out of here, replaced the ceiling."

"Yeah, I meant to get to it today, but unfortunately someone else had other ideas for me."

"I could maybe help you on Saturday. Kids got a soccer game I want to go to, but then we could knock the rest of it down, sheetrock, tape, and paint a first coat."

"Oh, thanks, man, I appreciate it. Let's see how things go tomorrow. I still have hopes for a date with Chastity."

"Good luck, man. Just don't mention me," he said, then picked up the dining room chair and walked out of the room.

I checked my computer one last time for a message from Chastity, drew a blank, then headed up to bed.

Thirty-six

Chastity responded to my email with, "I would sure _love_ a nooner!" I was up a little before eight. Farrell appeared to have been long gone. I showered, pulled the sheets off my bed because I could still detect Darcy's perfume, got the washer going, let Morton out, had breakfast, and then turned on my computer and saw her email.

I sent her a reply, *"Tell me where I can pick you up."*

She replied with a link to send a hundred dollar credit card payment. Once I sent the payment, she replied almost immediately with the pick-up place, followed by the line, *"Can't wait!"*

Apparently, she could wait, or at least she wasn't in any hurry. I was supposed to meet her on the corner of University and Jackson at high noon. That was twenty-five minutes ago, and she hadn't arrived yet. It was an intersection with stoplights, so two busy streets where I couldn't very well park.

I kept circling the block until I thought I might be getting dizzy. She had a description of my car, the 2007 Dodge Caliber. The official name of the car's color was

Sunburst Orange Pearl. I'd just told Chastity it was faded red with some rust spots over the wheel wells. There was a sticker on the rear bumper from the previous owner that read, "I brake for Bigfoot," but I didn't see the need to mention that at the time. Now, circling the block yet one more time, I was beginning to wonder.

It was just about my thousandth time around the block, and I was getting ready to hurry home and contact my credit card company when I saw her on the corner. It was like she'd suddenly appeared out of nowhere, and I wondered if she'd maybe just been dropped off or had parked in one of the paid lots right across the street.

I slowed down at the corner, lowered my window, and called, "Hey, Chastity."

The guy behind me leaned on his horn as she smiled and climbed in. I couldn't really blame him. I made a right turn, and fortunately, he continued straight ahead, still leaning on the horn. Chastity looked over the seat and out the back window.

"What an absolute asshole," she said, then glanced over at me and said, "Not you, I think you're nice. I meant that jerk honking his horn."

"Yeah, just trying to give a pretty girl a ride, and he gets all upset."

Her hair was bleached blonde, and I was thinking it looked a lot whiter than the last time I saw her in the parking lot of the Tryst Hotel watching Farrell drive away. She was definitely older-looking than her photo on the escort site, but that wasn't surprising. My car quickly filled with the eye-watering fumes from her perfume. She had blue eyes, heavy mascara, and a space between her two front teeth.

"Mmm-mmm. Say, you look kind of familiar. We date before?"

"No, I don't think so, unless you were working under a different name. Friend of mine said you were really good, and so I decided to give you a try."

"Oh really, who was that?"

"Well, he asked me not to pass his name on, he's kind of, how would I put it, in a sensitive position."

"That doesn't narrow it down much. Politician, cop, no, wait, I bet he's a priest? Yeah, that's it, a priest."

"I'd rather not say."

"Where we going, or do you just want to do me in the car?"

"Actually, I was thinking we'd just get acquainted. Maybe I could buy you lunch or something and—"

"Hey, look, let me explain something. You just drive and try to pay attention to what I say. You paid me a hundred bucks, that gets you an hour start to finish, okay. I mean time is money, no offense. You've already burned up about ten minutes of that time. See what I'm saying? You picking up what I'm putting down?"

"Yeah, I get that, in fact, that works fine for me. I just wanted to talk is all."

"Okay, who do you want me to be, your mother? A sister? I can be a really good kindergarten teacher."

"No, nothing like that. Actually, I wondered if you knew another girl, see—"

"Three-way is gonna cost you more, but yeah, I can do it. Might take thirty minutes or so to line someone up. What are you looking for, a blonde, or maybe a red—?"

"No, nothing like that. I wondered if you knew one of the other girls on the website."

"You a cop?

"Not exactly."

"Not exactly? What the hell is that supposed to mean? Tell you what, you have a nice day and just pull over and let me out."

"Hey, Chastity, relax, will you? I'm a private eye. Someone I know is looking for a girl who up until recently, maybe three or four months back, went by the name of Cherri. I think she was Canadian, had a big tattoo on—"

"Yeah, right above her ass, some hockey team or something. Yeah, I know her, or, knew of her. Never worked with her. Tried to pair up a couple of times, but it never worked out. What's this guy want with her, anyway?"

"Oh, that's the crazy part. He's infatuated with her, has some jewelry or something he wants to give her, but now he can't seem to find her posting anywhere on the site."

"Night Kandy?"

"Yeah, the same site you're on."

"Well, I might know her, and then again, I might not. Maybe tell me what it's worth to you and I'll see if that might help my memory."

"What it's worth to me?" I said, taking the entrance onto Interstate 94 heading east and picking up speed. "I could maybe go another fifty bucks."

"Fifty bucks? You gotta be kidding me."

"Hey, listen, that'd be a hundred and fifty bucks for about twenty minutes of your time, and you get to keep your pants on."

She seemed to think about that for a moment, then said, "Let me see the fifty first."

"You don't trust me?"

"Mister, in my business, you'd be stupid to trust anyone. Fifty bucks, cash."

I shook my head, then reached into my pocket and pulled out my wallet. I opened it, pulled out three twenties, and handed them to her. "Here, little tip, for being so understanding and willing to help."

She felt the bills between her thumb and forefinger, checking, I guess, to see if they felt legit. She folded the bills and stuffed them into her bra. "Okay, like I said, I don't actually know her. She went by a couple of names. Cherri is the one I remember. Pretty popular, least as far as I know."

"You know how I, or actually my client, can get hold of her? Like I said, she seems to be off the site."

She shook her head, "Girl like that, she may have left town. Little I knew, I always suspected she was just here for a certain amount of time before she was off to somewhere else, Vegas, Florida, California, Washington, that's D.C., where the big money is. Who the hell knows?"

"You gotta have some idea, or maybe someone else I could contact who might know."

She raised her eyebrows. "No one better than me, baby, and I'm not just talking in the sack."

"Then prove it."

"I'm getting to that, God, but you're a crabby one. She seemed to be a regular at Cheaters."

"Cheaters? That strip club?"

"Yeah, it's a halfway decent pick-up place if one of us is having a slow night. A lot of guys *on the way home* as we say."

"Cheaters?"

"Yeah, but now I haven't heard hide nor hair of her for a while, so take it with a grain of salt. Honestly, I don't know of anyone else I could send you to."

"Okay. Thanks. One more question, and then we'll head back on the next exit. You were with a guy about a week or two ago. He left you over in Wisconsin, I think, and—"

"That idiot Stud Muffin One? What the hell was his name? I'm trying to think. Farrell?"

"I think it was something like that. Can't remember exactly," I lied.

"What about him? I tell you, if I ever see him again, it'd be too soon. How'd you hear about that?"

"Someone else I was talking to said they heard it from someone. Said the guy never got his money's worth."

"If you mean did we do anything, the answer is no. He just sat there in a chair and kept apologizing. I finally went to sleep, or at least tried to. Never even had my clothes off. Tell you the truth, I was afraid that idiot might kill me or something, so yeah, it was a pain in the butt getting home, but then again I'm here to tell the story. Can't say I was all that upset in the end to see him drive off. Bit of a nutcase, that one."

"Appreciate your help, Chastity," I said, taking the exit, crossing over the interstate and then heading back into town. "Any place special you'd like me to drop you off?"

"No, I think just near where you picked me up will be fine. Listen, you ever need a little loving, you be sure to give me a call. I'll give you the gold card discount," she said and smiled.

Thirty-seven

The music in Cheaters was lousy, really lousy. If you were supposed to recognize the songs, I was way out of it. I hadn't recognized one tune, and I'd been sitting there for the better part of three hours nursing a beer, the same beer. I wasn't enjoying the evening.

There'd been a bit of a spurt to the crowd, say for about an hour and a half starting around five. But now it was after eight and the crowd had thinned substantially. The mood of the dancers on stage seemed to reflect that. They all looked bored and seemed to focus on some distant point I don't think anyone in the place was going to see. Smiles from the dancers and the wait staff seemed to be a rare occurrence.

My waitress was dressed in one of those French maid type of outfits with a little lace thing on her head, and a frilly apron that I guess was supposed to look sexy, only her outfit was a half-dozen sizes too big. Even in the dark, the thing looked faded, more grey than black, and a seam along the side, just under her armpit, was torn for maybe a couple of inches. Her face was drawn, and the bags under her eyes suggested she hadn't slept in a week or two. Her hair was pulled up in a half-hearted bun that seemed to be slowly coming undone.

"Another beer, honey?" she asked.

"No, this one is just fine," I said. My glass was still half full, and the beer was warm, now more flat than not. I quickly scanned the room, looking for Darcy, but didn't see anyone even close. A blonde at the bar caught my eye for a moment, raised her eyebrows suggestively, and gave me a slight nod.

"Two drink minimum to sit at the table, sir, otherwise I'm afraid you'll have to take a stool over at the bar. These seats are in high demand."

I glanced around the area. Close to half the tables were empty. Two of the tables had guys in some animated discussions, laughing and hitting one another on the shoulder, doing everything but paying attention to the bored, naked women slowly dancing on stage.

"High demand for these tables?"

She gave a tired sounding sigh, looked around for a brief moment, then said, "Hey, it's what they told me I have to say. I need the job, so what can I do except tell you the tables are in high demand."

"Let me ask you something. You know a girl who comes here once in a while? She's on an escort site, goes by the name Cherri. I think she might be Canadian. Dark hair, fairly attractive."

"You a cop?"

"No, trying to find her for a friend of mine. He had a date with her a while back. Guess she's off the escort site now, but he'd like to link up with her again. Said she was a lot of fun. I guess she had a big tattoo—"

"Oh, yeah, maybe. That tattoo right above her ass? A hockey team, right?

"Montreal Canadiens."

"Yeah, that's right, she's Canadian. She'd dance here once in a while on amateur night. Nice enough, I guess, but kind of private. Not sure she ever won amateur night."

I pulled a ten out of my pocket, laid it on the table then pushed it toward her. "I know her as Cherri, but I think that's just a name she uses, probably not her real name."

"To be honest, now that I think about it, I don't believe I ever heard anyone call her by her name. She seemed to work out of here once in a while if you kind of get my drift. They usually sit in that back corner of the bar, maybe take a long look at someone before approaching. I'm sure they have to give the bartenders a percentage, I don't know how much, but I have to pay fifteen percent just to wait tables."

I hoped the surprise on my face didn't show. I couldn't believe the line would be too long to do anything except leave her alone. She gave a quick look around, then snatched up the ten and slipped it into a pocket in her apron. "Thanks. It's still a two-drink minimum for the table, and it don't look that way now, but it'll fill up in here around half past nine once the softball games are over, then it gets crazy."

I gave her my glass of flat beer and said thanks, then made my way over to the bar area and settled onto a stool.

Thirty-eight

The waitress hadn't been kidding. No more than twenty minutes later, a steady stream of guys started coming through the door, and a half-hour after that, the place was pretty much standing room only. Most of the clientele were in softball jerseys, different teams from all ends of town. The majority of guys looked like they were just out for the night with pals. A few looked to be stopping for just one on their way home, and a couple of guys looked like they were in the market for some very personal attention.

The vibe from the dancers had improved about a thousand percent. Most of the seats along the stage were filled, and stacks of dollar bills sat in front of a number of the occupants. The dancers seemed to be more than willing to earn their tips.

Even I was starting to enjoy the atmosphere a little more. I was on my second beer while sitting at the bar, and now I recognized maybe half the songs playing for the dancers.

There were three women sitting in the darkest corner of the bar. They had left a stool or two between them and appeared to be on their own. None of them was

Darcy. I'd made eye contact with two of them. Not intentionally, it just kind of happened, and I was debating whether it would be worth the effort to ask them if they knew her.

Two guys in softball jerseys entered and headed toward a crowd of a half-dozen similarly dressed individuals. Then, before the door had completely closed, it opened again and in she walked, Darcy.

I actually hunched down and put a hand up to the side of my face, hoping she wouldn't recognize me and run out the door. She seemed to scan the room for a moment, then walked along the far side of the bar and into the ladies' room. I hurried out to my car, pulled out of my parking place, did a quick spin through the lot, then drifted into the back end of the lot and waited.

I was in the darkest corner of the lot. There was an old, rusty pickup filled with recyclable items on one side of me and a dumpster on the other. It was almost ten.

I'd been parked next to the dumpster for what felt like a week and checked the time once again on my phone. Now it was just a little after midnight, and I had been fighting the urge to use the restroom, any restroom. Three beers were starting to take their toll, but I was afraid if I went inside, Darcy would see me and either run or call Fatty and his friend for backup. The way my luck ran, if I drove over to the gas station just across the intersection, that would be exactly the moment Darcy would come out the door and head home or wherever she was going. So I waited, and then waited some more.

Now it was almost one in the morning, and the crowd inside Cheaters was definitely thinning, getting down to just the hardcore. Unfortunately, the place advertised in red neon letters that flashed off and on above the door that it was open until two, seven nights a week, 365 days a year. I could only hope I'd make it another hour.

I finally couldn't wait any longer. I climbed out of my car, groaned with the pain of needing to relieve myself after all the beer, and made my way behind the dumpster. The street light was a half block away, and I couldn't see any headlights coming in either direction, plus I was just out of time.

God, the relief. I think I was standing back there for four or five minutes. At least it felt that long. Not a complaint, by the way. I waited an extra minute just to make sure I was finished, gave a long, final sigh of relief, zipped up, and headed back to my car.

The blow to the back of my head was anything but subtle. I remember seeing a pair of black jeans on my way down, and I think I heard car tires screeching, maybe.

Thirty-nine

I bounced around inside the car trunk for a good twenty minutes before we began to slow. Up until now, the movement of the car and the sounds from the wheels suggested we were traveling on a fairly major street. It hadn't felt like we'd been speeding down an interstate, but we weren't creeping down a quiet side street either.

Eventually, we stopped, and I heard a sound I presumed was some kind of garage door opening. The car moved forward just a bit, stopped, and a moment later, the engine was turned off. I heard more conversation, at least two voices, male and female, but I still couldn't make out what was being said. Car doors opened and closed, and the voices grew distant before they faded away altogether.

I was half curled up, lying on my side in the dark. I remained in the trunk of the vehicle for what seemed like a very long time. I had a lump on the back of my head that was throbbing, and my hands were bound at the wrists and then somehow attached to my waist so that I couldn't really move them. It was all very uncomfortable, to say the least.

I heard what sounded like a door opening, then footsteps and faint voices that gradually grew louder. What sounded like the car door opened, and then the lid to the trunk suddenly popped up. A hand appeared and raised the trunk lid all the way open. Two pairs of hands reached in and unceremoniously pulled me out of the trunk, banging my head against the open lid in the process. Fatty and his friend, and they didn't look all that happy to see me.

"Ouch, God, take it easy, I'm not going anywhere. Jesus Christ, that hurt. You two guys should—"

"Please, just shut up, for your own damn good," Fatty said.

Actually, that sounded like pretty sage advice. They walked me across the garage toward a door, holding me with a firm hand on either arm. It was a double garage, mostly empty except for the black Mercedes they'd pulled me out of. There were two cardboard boxes stacked near the side door, but that was it. Otherwise, the place looked unused.

We took a step up to the grey metal door and entered a small entryway with the front door just to the left, a bifold door straight ahead and a set of about eight steps leading up to what looked like a living room and kitchen off to the right. I could just make out a refrigerator door parked inside the entrance to the kitchen.

The skinny guy pulled the bifold doors open. Then they angled and pushed me into the small closet and closed the doors behind me. I had to stand hunched over because there was a clothes bar and a shelf in there at just about my shoulder height. The only thing in the closet was a striped pair of what looked like heavy slipper socks. It sounded like they attached something to the knobs on the outside of the doors, then one of them gave the doors a couple of tugs to see if they would open. They didn't.

A voice said something in French, not sounding all that friendly, and then the voice faded as they walked up the stairs.

With the light shining through the slats in the bifold doors, I could make out some black cloth tied around my wrists. My arms were held tight against my sides by what looked like a belt. I suddenly realized it was my belt, only because my initials were engraved in the back of the thing, meaning the buckle was up against my spine.

I wiggled, angled, twisted back and forth, banged my head on the damn shelf a half-dozen times, and finally inched the belt up my chest. Now I could bend my arms at the elbows. I reached up and grabbed the belt between my thumb and index fingers then slowly worked the thing around, a quarter-inch at a time until the buckle was centered on my chest. Once the buckle was centered, it wasn't that difficult to inch the end of the belt out of the silver tab, then pull the belt back until the buckle became undone. That allowed me to move my arms more or less freely. Working with my fingers and mouth, I gradually loosened the knot on the cloth binding my wrists enough to slip one wrist from beneath the black cloth, and in short order, I had the damn cloth off my wrists.

I was in the process of studying the bifold doors. I could probably just kick through the things enough to escape, but Fatty or his skinny pal would most likely be down here before I'd done enough damage to get out. I gently pushed against the doors, and they stopped moving after no more than half an inch, obviously, they were somehow secured from the outside.

I was examining the spring-loaded pins on the top of the doors that kept them on the track as they were opened or closed when I heard a noise coming from the other side that sounded an awful lot like footsteps stomping down the carpeted stairway.

A moment later, I heard the beeping sound of someone inputting a code into a keypad, and I guessed whoever was out there was setting the alarm for the night.

I grabbed my belt from the floor and quickly wrapped it around my right fist, letting the large silver buckle hang loose by a good four inches. Something tugged at the bifold doors right where I guessed the knobs to be, and a half-second later, the doors swung open. I jumped out of the closet and swung with all my might cracking the heavy silver buckle into the side of the skinny guy's head.

He let off half a groan, but that was cut short when I backhanded the buckle across his mouth. I swung hard again, thunking the buckle off the side of his head, and he sunk to his knees. I grabbed him by the hair, pulled his head forward, and slammed my knee into his face a number of times, as fast and hard as I could, until he seemed to grow limp. I lowered him to the floor and saw that he was bleeding profusely from his nose and mouth. I searched him, found a pistol tucked into his belt at the small of his back, then rolled him onto his stomach and used the black cloth they'd tied me up with to bind his hands behind his back. I dragged and rolled him into the closet, stuffed one of the heavy slipper socks into his mouth, then closed the door and secured it with the childproof lock that had held the door closed just a moment earlier when I had been confined.

If he was going to get out, he'd have to kick the door open, which would hopefully give me enough of a warning. I debated whether I should just go out the door and make a run for it, but then I remembered Colleen Lacy and set off to look for her.

Forty

Next to the door that led to the attached garage was a short hallway with four doors. I slowly crept down the hall. The first door was partially open and led to a laundry room, empty except for the washer and dryer. The door across the hall from that was a small bathroom with just a toilet and sink. The door in the left corner of the hall was closed, and I listened for what seemed like a very long time to see if I could hear any noise from inside. After what seemed like an hour, I slowly opened the door and peeked into an empty room. Absolutely nothing was in there, not so much as a wastebasket.

I listened at the door immediately across the hall, but again, couldn't hear anything. I waited for another very long time before I cautiously turned the knob and ever so slowly pushed the door open. It was dark in the room, but I could make out two fairly large windows in the upper half of one wall. A cheap curtain or maybe a bed sheet had been drawn over the windows. I remained still and waited for my eyes to adjust. Gradually, I could make out rumpled sheets and a pillow on an empty single bed. A dresser standing in a far corner of the room slowly took shape. What looked like a small suitcase lay open on the floor next to the dresser. I looked around as best I could and was about to close the door when I heard what sounded like a sigh or maybe a throat being cleared. It came from the corner where the bed was, but there was no one on the bed.

I waited and watched for the longest time and eventually thought I could hear breathing. Deep breathing, like someone asleep.

I slowly entered the room on all fours, headed toward the noise. It was now sounding very steady, regular, and coming from under the bed. As I drew closer I could make out a foot lying on the carpet beneath the bed, next to the bedpost, the more I stared, the more I could begin to see a pair of feet.

I crawled alongside the bed, looked carefully and saw a wrist and hand next to the bedpost, and then realized the wrist was bound to the post with what looked like a silk tie. The kind of tie some guy might wear to the office. Whoever was under there, they'd been tied to the bed frame.

I stretched out, cautiously reached in under the bed, and placed my hand where I thought the head would be. I had placed my hand over someone's nose and quickly moved it down to cover the mouth just as they started to make a noise. I applied some pressure.

"Shhh-shhh, be quiet. I want to untie you and get you out of here. Do you understand?"

I think they nodded.

"I'm going to take my hand off and untie you. Don't make a sound. Please," I said, then slowly pulled my hand away. I quickly reached over and untied the wrist, then crawled down to the end of the bed and untied the ankle. I crawled over to the bedpost closest to the wall and untied the other ankle, then climbed onto the bed and reached down to untie the other wrist, but it was gone, and just a silk tie lay on the rug. A moment later, a figure rolled out from beneath the bed.

It was a woman, at least I thought it was a woman, dressed in what looked like a grey sweatsuit. She rolled out onto the floor, then half-sat up and arched her back, stretching it. She reached up and pulled a blindfold from her eyes so that it hung loosely around her neck and leaned forward. She began shaking her hands and wiggling her fingers as she looked up at me.

"God, Dev, am I ever glad to see you!"

"Colleen? What the hell? Come on, let's get out of here."

"You don't have to tell me twice," she said. I rolled off the bed and helped her to her feet, then put my index finger to my lips, signaling quiet before I led her out of the room. There was some noise beginning to come from the closet, a muffled groan. I was tempted to open the closet door and whack the guy over the head with his pistol. Instead, I stopped at the door leading into the garage. The house alarm keypad was mounted on the wall next to the door, and a light on the keypad was blinking.

A digital readout that read "ARMED" flashed off and on.

"When I open this door, the alarm is probably going to sound," I whispered. "This leads to the garage. We'll go out here, then out of the garage, and we can hide in a neighbor's yard. You going to be able to do that?"

We heard another groan, this time a little louder, followed by something brushing against one of the bifold doors like the guy had maybe kneed it just to see if it might open.

"You can follow me."

"You just try and keep up," Colleen whispered back. "Come on let's get the hell out of here."

Another groan, this one even louder than before, and what sounded like a definite kick against the bifold door turned out to be all the incentive we needed to be on our way.

Forty-one

I tore open the door leading to the garage. The alarm system began beeping, not loud, but just giving off the warning you'd get to remind one you forgot to disarm the alarm. I figured thirty seconds at the most. We headed toward the overhead garage door. A green light next to the door identified the button to push that would raise the door. Just as I pushed the button and the door began to rise, the alarm went off, this time for real. The sound was deafening.

As soon as the garage door had risen high enough so we could duck beneath it, Colleen shot past me, ducked under the door, and took off down the driveway. I waited half a step, then ducked beneath the door, stopped, and fired the pistol into both rear tires of the Mercedes. I followed Colleen down the driveway. There was a car parked out on the street, some BMW, blue with a red convertible top. I didn't know whose it was, so I put two more rounds into those rear tires and tried to catch up to Colleen. I had to run all out past three houses before I caught up to her. I glanced over my shoulder and saw the hint of a light on in an upstairs window of the house we'd just fled. I didn't know if the light had been on all the time or if it had just come on, and I wasn't about to go back and find out.

"Lights on down the street, head for those," I said, too winded to say anything else.

God knows where she got it from, but Colleen actually picked up speed and took off down the block. We cut across two front lawns and ran through a flower patch in front of the house with the lights on. Colleen rang the doorbell, and when I finally caught up to her, I began pounding on the door, I continued pounding for a very long time.

Eventually, I saw a woman through the glass panel next to the door cautiously approaching. She had a fleece blanket wrapped around her shoulders, appeared to be wearing a nightie, and she was barefoot. She stared at us from behind her front door but didn't open the door. I couldn't really blame her, it had to be around three in the morning.

"Please, call the police," I said.

"The police call them. We were kidnapped," Colleen said, and the woman ran back into the room she'd just come from. We remained out on the front porch, nervously watching down the street for any movement for a good ten minutes before we heard first one siren and then another.

"Thank God," Colleen said.

A moment later, a squad car pulled in front of the house, and a cop got out of the car. The other siren was definitely growing louder, but it wasn't on the street yet.

I shoved the pistol in the back of my belt, and we headed toward the squad car at the curb. The lights on top were still flashing, and the cop yelled, "Stop right there. Put your hands up." He had his gun drawn, and he was crouched down behind the hood of the squad car.

"It's okay, we're the victims here," Colleen said and started to hurry toward him.

I grabbed her by the arm and said, "He can't be sure. Just do as he says. He's probably going to ask us to turn around and walk backward toward him."

"But we didn't do—"

"Stop right where you are. Place your hands over your head."

"Just do it, Colleen," I said and raised my hands over my head, thankfully she followed suit.

"Now, I want you to turn around and walk toward me, backward."

"I'm going to do that," I said. "But when I turn, you're going to see a pistol stuffed in my belt, right in the small of my back," I said. I noticed a pair of headlights racing up the street toward us. Thankfully there were flashing lights on the top of the car, another cop. We turned then walked backward toward the street.

"All right, stop right there. Do not turn around."

"This is so stupid," Colleen said, but she stopped.

We could hear voices behind us and another siren in the distance. They seemed to be discussing something. Finally, someone called, "Sir, I need you to kneel down and then lay face down on the ground. Do not turn round. Keep your hands above your head at all times."

I knelt down, then stretched out on the ground. I noticed the upstairs light had come on in the house where I'd pounded on the door as well as both houses on either side.

"Ma'am, I want you to move about five steps to your right, keep your hands above your head at all times, then kneel down and lay face down on the ground."

I heard another car door slam, and a moment later, footsteps coming up behind me.

"There's a pistol tucked into the small of my back," I said and was thinking I didn't get a response when just a second later, I felt a knee in my back and the pistol was pulled out of my belt. My arms were pulled back, and I was handcuffed.

The same thing must have been done to Colleen because I heard her half scream, and then she said, "Did you listen to anything we said? I just got done telling you we were kidnapped. We escaped from that house up the street. The one with the French guys. We told that woman to call you, for God's sake. Ouch, hey, watch it, are you guys crazy? Are you even listening? I'm telling you, they're going to get away. Did you even hear what I just said?"

Forty-two

I was still handcuffed, but at least they'd put me in the back of one of the squad cars, and I wasn't lying face down in someone's front yard. I'd been sitting in the car for a good thirty minutes. Probably a half-dozen cop cars were now parked up and down the street. People were out on their front porches wearing bathrobes, and one fat guy was just in his boxers.

I could see Colleen talking to two of the cops. Suddenly a familiar figure entered the circle, Aaron LaZelle. He spoke to Colleen for a brief moment, then said something to one of the cops, who hurried over to the car I was sitting in and opened the backdoor.

"Sorry about that, Mr. Haskell. We just had to get things checked out. If you want to climb out, I can get those cuffs off you right away. Umm, I guess the Lieutenant would like to talk to you," he said. He placed a hand on the top of my head as I swung my feet out of the car and onto the ground. He carefully pulled me to my feet so I wouldn't bump my head on the doorframe, then said, "Turn around, and we'll get those cuffs off. Good, okay," he said as I heard a click, and one of my wrists was suddenly free.

He undid the other cuff, then said, "Lieutenant LaZelle is right over there with those other folks. He'd like to talk with you."

I hurried over to the group. Aaron was just saying to Colleen, "Two guys and a woman, three people. No one else?"

"No, I've told this to the other officers. Look, they're going to get away. Probably have by now. You need to get down there right now and—"

"Aaron, she's right. They've had a half-hour head start to pack up and go. You need to—"

"We've got people in the front and back watching. The alarm has been turned off, and the vehicles are still in the garage and in front of the house. So—"

"That's because I shot out the rear tires on both vehicles. Even if they change the tire, they'd still have a flat. Not that they'd want to take the time."

Aaron's eyes grew wide, and he clicked on the radio he held in his hand, turned from me and said something into the radio I couldn't understand.

At that moment, a pair of large headlights pulled onto the street at the far end of the block and headed our way. Red and blue lights on the front of the vehicle were flashing, but there was no siren. As it drew closer, I could make out the silhouette of a dark industrial van. The vehicle stopped in the middle of the street, and Aaron ran over just as the rear doors opened up. He shouted something to a guy climbing out of the passenger seat and suddenly a dozen, maybe more guys, all dressed in black with protective vests, helmets, knee and elbow pads, and automatic weapons rushed out of the van. Words were quickly exchanged, and a moment later, they all hurried down the street toward the house we'd fled.

"Dev," Aaron called and motioned me forward with his hand. I hurried over to him. The armed cops, I guess the SWAT team, were almost down the block, and a handful of guys looked to be cutting through some yards heading toward the back of the house. "The Lacy woman said there were three people, two men, and a woman."

"Yeah, it was that Darcy gal and the two guys who broke into my place the other night, same ones who taped me to the chair. But I didn't get much past the ground floor. I don't know if there were more people upstairs asleep or what. They had me in the trunk of the car, but I heard their voices."

"What an absolute cluster fuck."

"Yeah, I'd say there's a pretty good chance they're long gone."

"Well, we're going to find out shortly."

"Let me go with you."

He studied me for a long moment, then said, "Okay, but you do as you're told. I got nervous people with weapons. I don't need you running off and getting in the way."

"Believe me, I've got no intention of doing anything like that."

We headed off down the street. A car was parked in the driveway across the street from the house where I'd been held. The house was dark. In fact, all the homes around the house I'd been held in were dark. Even the porch lights were off. I guessed the residents had probably been evacuated out the back, or they were hunkered down in their basements.

Two cops had a couple of computers hooked up sitting on the hood of the parked car in the driveway. We hurried alongside them, and Aaron said, "Anything?"

"Cold, no image. We're going to do a third run through, just to be sure, but we're coming up empty inside."

"The rear tires on both vehicles were flattened," Aaron said.

"Yeah, that's what we heard."

The cop looked over at me and said, "Nice work."

The house across the street looked dark, with the exception of the light in the second-floor corner room that I'd seen earlier. The garage door was up, and the light was on in the garage so you could see the Mercedes. From where we crouched across the street, we couldn't really tell that the rear tires were flat on the car.

We knelt down in front of the vehicle while they ran through another check, looking for heat sources that would indicate someone in the house. After some time, they came up empty-handed. Aaron got on the radio, had a couple of short back and forth words with someone, then said, "Okay, they'll be going in, in just a moment. Soon as we get the all-clear from them, we can head in."

As he spoke, we watched two groups of crouched figures move along either side of the front of the house. Two guys peeled off and positioned themselves in the garage just behind the Mercedes. At least six people were at the front door with a battering ram thing. They waited a moment then suddenly swung the battering ram. There was a loud noise, almost like an explosion, as the front door flew wide open, and everyone charged in.

"Police, police," they yelled as they stormed into the house with their weapons pointed. Three guys headed off to the right, down the short hall where I'd found Colleen Lacy under the bed, while the rest charged up the staircase. Gradually we could see lights coming on in various rooms in the house.

It was all over in about three minutes. Aaron got an "All Clear" call on his radio, and we headed across the street to the house while the two cops began to pack up their computers resting on the hood of the car.

"What do you hope to find in here?" I asked as we headed up the driveway.

"What I hope to find is all three of these bastards, handcuffed and begging to talk. My fear is that in reality, we're going to find an empty house that was hastily left. Which means that at this stage of the game . . ." He checked his watch. "They could have walked, run, grabbed a taxi, or even an Uber ride and be just about anywhere."

Forty-three

One thing was for sure, they weren't in the house. With the exception of the small, open suitcase I saw in the basement bedroom, a larger one in an upstairs corner bedroom, and four coffee cups in the sink, there wasn't much to suggest someone had been in the house.

I showed Aaron the closet with the bifold doors. There was a good deal of blood on the carpet in the closet, way more than I thought there would be, and I could only hope that the thin guy I hit over the head with my belt buckle was experiencing one hell of a headache.

There was no sign of Demarcus. Anywhere. We did find the boxes of pigment that Demarcus had used to mix his various colors, the same boxes the French guys had packed up and taken from my house. There were twenty-two splatter canvases stacked up against a wall. Remnants of two of the canvases were crumpled up and looked to have been hurriedly tossed in a corner.

"Someone finally came to their senses and began to destroy those dreadful things," I said, looking at the two canvases crumpled up in the corner.

Aaron pursed his lips and seemed to be thinking.

"Don't worry, Aaron, it's not rare art. It's a bunch of crap is what it is."

He picked up one of the splattered canvases from the stack and pulled out a small knife from his pocket. He took the knife and wedged out some staples on either side of a frame, then slowly pulled the canvas back, maybe six or eight inches.

"Oh, Jesus Christ, will you look at this. Bingo. This is what it's all been about."

"What?"

"Everything. God, right in front of us the whole time, and we never caught on. Your break-in, Darcy, or whoever in the hell she really is, the kidnapping, look at this," he said and held the canvas out for me to take a look.

Below the splatter work that any kindergarten kid could have done was the corner of a painting with vibrant tones, and what appeared to be a foot.

"What the hell?"

"The Interpol warning about the forgeries. Here they are. Probably a painting beneath every one of these splattered pieces of shit, and we never even thought to check. That's what they were after. Remember what that Darcy was telling us about the canvas? Didn't she test it and say it was at least a hundred and twenty-five years old? Dev, there's a forgery under every one of these things on antique canvas. It's what your close friend Demarcus has been doing for the past four or five months.

It's why he wanted you to get these things from Colleen Lacy before she burned them."

Aaron did a quick count of the canvases. "There's twenty-two of these things. Didn't you think they took twenty-four?"

"Well, yeah, but I can't be sure of that number. What are you thinking, they ran out of here with just two? If that was the case, the three of them, those two guys and Darcy, why not grab three or six? And then, that said, how would they even know which one of these would be the most valuable?"

"Maybe they didn't know. Maybe they had no idea. Maybe you and Colleen escaping brought everything to a sudden, screeching halt. They're going to load up the paintings, but the tires are flat on the cars, they've gotta run for it, and now we're talking minutes rather than hours. They hear the sirens, panic, and they grab the two closest paintings and flee the scene."

One of the cops from the SWAT team stepped into the room, did a quick glance at the splatter painting Aaron held, and wrinkled his nose in disgust. "God. Hey, Lieutenant, you might want to come take a look at this. We got a body out in the garage."

Forty-four

We followed him down the staircase, past the closet with the bifold doors. There was a guy kneeling in front of the closet, taking pictures of the blood on the carpet. The door leading out to the garage was open, and we followed our guy to the back of the Mercedes. The lid to the trunk was up, and I could just catch a glimpse of a body lying inside. Two guys in hazmat suits were there, apparently fingerprinting the guy and taking his temperature. Outside there were a number of cops in a line slowly walking back and forth across the lawn with flashlights.

Two small, yellow plastic tents maybe four inches tall, with the numbers one and two on them were out in the driveway next to two brass shell casings.

"Hey, Aaron, those shell casings they've identified, they're probably from the rounds I put into the rear tires on this Mercedes. There should be two more out by that BMW convertible parked in the street. I shot the tires out on that, too."

"You still have the weapon?"

"No, those cops up the street took it from me when they arrived. I grabbed it from one of the French guys."

Aaron looked around, then called a guy over. "Hey, Greg, there should be two more shell casings out by that car in the street. Dev, where were you when you fired?"

"Right at the end of the driveway, maybe three or four feet behind the car."

"Mark 'em, okay?" Aaron said as the guy hurried down the driveway.

The two guys in the hazmat suits stepped back from the trunk of the Mercedes a couple of minutes later, and Aaron and I stepped forward. The face on the body was battered. The left eye was bruised, the right side of the guy's lips were swollen and split. There was a vicious wound on the left side of his skull, above the temple, where the skin was split for about two inches. Blood from the wound was dried along the side of his face. It was the tall, thin French guy, and the beating he'd received had been compliments of my silver belt buckle. But he had been alive when last I saw him. I had nothing to do with the bullet hole just above his right eye.

"That's the guy I stuffed into the closet, the bastard. I attacked him with my belt buckle when he opened the bifold door to check on me. But I didn't shoot him."

"You sure?" Aaron asked. "Looks like fairly close range."

"Yeah, it does, but the pistol I took from him was at least a nine-millimeter, it would have blown the back of his head off. My guess, it was either the fat man or Darcy. The alarm goes off, they run down the stairs just as he kicks the closet door open, or they come around the corner upstairs just as he's coming out of the closet, and they shoot him. That's probably why they only took two paintings. Maybe they were standing by the door ready to turn off the alarm. He surprises them coming out of the closet, they shoot, dump his body in the trunk so they won't leave any evidence, and then notice that the tires are flat. They figure they've got about ninety seconds to grab a painting and get the hell out of here before the cops show up. Just in case they have any doubts, they hear sirens, so they just take off on foot."

"And they confiscated the weapon you had?"

"Yeah, the cops you were talking to when you first arrived took it."

"Okay, I'll have them bring it down here. We'll want to do a ballistics test."

"That explains all the blood on the carpet in that closet. It maybe makes sense, the alarm going off, Fatty flies downstairs just as this asshole kicks the bifold doors open. Fatty probably points and fires more as a reaction than actually aiming, and he hits the guy in the forehead, kills him."

"Yeah, possibly. I'm wondering, there were four coffee mugs up in the kitchen sink. Does that mean someone else was here? Maybe Demarcus? Maybe he's our shooter, and he chased the other two out of here."

"Demarcus? He wouldn't do that, would he?"

"Humf, all in all, I'd call it a pretty bad night."

"At least for this guy," I said and nodded at the body in the trunk of the Mercedes.

"Got 'em, Lieutenant," the cop called from the base of the driveway. He was placing two more of the little yellow plastic tents just a couple of feet behind the BMW out on the street.

"You check for any ID?" Aaron asked one of the guys in the hazmat suit.

"Went over his pockets. Couldn't be absolutely sure, but they felt empty. We'll be going in there in a few minutes. We find anything, we'll let you know."

Aaron nodded, then said, "Come on, let's go back upstairs. I want to check out those canvases."

We headed back upstairs to the corner bedroom. Aaron pulled on a pair of blue latex gloves just as we entered the room. He took the small knife from his pocket and picked up one of the splattered canvases. I went to reach for a canvas, and he said, "Better not, Dev. I don't want your fingerprints contaminating the evidence."

"You kidding? I stacked these damn things in my guest room, after carrying them up to my second floor. My prints are probably all over them."

"Just stand over there and humor me. This will only take a moment," he said, then began to pry the staples loose from the wooden frame the canvas was attached to. In less than two minutes, he'd loosened the canvas around the corner of the painting and pulled it back, revealing the vibrant tones of another painting underneath. He set the painting over against the far wall, then picked up the next canvas and repeated the procedure. Another painting was underneath, and so it went for all of the remaining canvases.

"A painting underneath every one of these things. I'm guessing if we check the ones left behind at your place, we won't find any," Aaron said.

"Which is why they took these. God, and all the while I thought he was just wasting his time and talent on a lost cause, all those splattered pieces of shit."

"He was way ahead of all of us. The question remains, where in the hell is he now?"

"Along with Darcy and that fat guy."

Forty-five

Aaron pulled to a stop next to the dumpster where I'd parked my car in the back of Cheaters parking lot.

"You sure this is where you parked?" he said, looking at the empty parking space next to the dumpster. As a matter of fact, virtually the entire lot was empty. It was just a little after 7:00 am and Cheaters didn't open for the noon crowd until 11:00.

I stepped out and gazed over the roof of the car, scanning the parking lot, hoping to see another dumpster with my worthless car parked next to it. I didn't.

"Yeah, unfortunately, I'm sure this is where I parked. Shit, I left my keys in the ignition when I stepped behind the dumpster to take a piss. Can you believe it, some jerk actually stole that thing?"

"You're talking about that 2007 thing? It was kind of a horse shit pinkish color, wasn't it?"

"It was a 2007 Dodge Caliber, Sunburst Orange Pearl, to be specific. It had maybe faded just a little. God, I can't believe someone ripped it off."

"Yeah, well, no one is more surprised than me. You see anyone hanging around while you were parked back here?"

"You kidding? It was almost one in the morning. No, the only people I saw were guys coming out of Cheaters and heading to their cars. I finally had to go so bad I could almost taste it. Next thing I know, I zip up, take about two steps, and boom, it's lights out. Then, I wake up in the trunk of that Mercedes and, well, you were there for most of the rest of it. Damn it." I looked up and down the street in a vain attempt to spot my car but didn't see anything that resembled it.

"Well, let's go, get back in, and I'll give you a lift home. You can file a report later today. Someone stealing that car has all the earmarks of a bunch of kids or a drunk taking it for a joy ride. It's probably sitting on a side street within a half-mile of here. Come on, I want to get down to the office and check on the BOLO we've got out on your girlfriend Darcy and her fat friend."

Aaron pulled to the curb in front of my place about fifteen minutes later. The morning rush hour was just beginning to pick up. "You got a way to get into your house?"

"Yeah, I got some keys stashed in back, at least I think they're still there. Just in case, can you hang tight for a minute? I'll let myself in the back, wave at you from the front door, then you can take off. Thanks for the lift."

"Not a problem. Thanks for finding Colleen Lacy. That's a big headache off my desk. We'll want you to come down and file a more formal report. I'll have someone give you a call, and we'll give you a ride down to the station."

"Someone give me a call? You mean like that pain in the ass, Manning?"

"Dev, he's just doing his job. Lighten up."

"Aaron, I've told you before. The guy has it in for me. He's going to try and find some obscure link and use it as a way to nail me for Colleen Lacy's kidnapping, believe me."

"Yeah, whatever. Go see if you can find those house keys so I can get back to work and accomplish something."

"Thanks again," I said, then hurried up my driveway. I had the keys hidden inside a fake pile of rubber dog pooh in a corner of the backyard. Fortunately, the fake pile and the keys were still there. I unlocked the backdoor and called Morton's name as I walked toward the front door. I opened the front door and gave Aaron a wave. He tooted his horn a couple of times and headed down the street. I called Morton's name again and heard a familiar thump upstairs in the bedroom. By the time I got up there, Morton was just finishing his stretching, and he came over and licked my hand.

"Come on, let's go outside," I said and hurried back downstairs. Morton took his time following. I had his food and water dish refilled by the time he made it into the kitchen. "Come on, boy, outside, Morton, outside." That seemed to get his tail wagging, and he bounded halfway to the backdoor and out into the backyard. I watched him for a minute, then headed upstairs and took a hot shower.

I let Morton back in, warmed some microwave pancakes which I inhaled, then sacked out on the couch. I woke an hour or two later with Morton licking my face, then went upstairs to my guest room. There was still a stack of paintings leaning against the wall, and I took a letter opener from the dresser and went through the same procedure that Aaron had done, loosening the staples from the frame around one corner and pulling the canvas back. I was halfway through the stack of canvases when Morton barked from downstairs in the living room, and a moment later, my doorbell rang.

I hurried downstairs and opened the front door to two policemen.

"Mr. Haskell, we're here to take you down for your statement regarding the Colleen Lacy kidnapping."

It suddenly dawned on me that my cellphone had been sitting on the passenger seat of my car, which meant my phone was wherever my car was unless the fool who stole it was using the thing.

"I'll be right with you. Let me just get some shoes on."

"Maybe some trousers, too," the officer said and nodded at my boxers.

"Shirt might be a good idea," the cop behind him said, and they both laughed.

Forty-six

I was seated in interview room three. I'd been in here more than a few times, usually under a lot less pleasant circumstances. Aaron was asking questions. A female detective by the name of Norah Demming was next to him taking notes. She was blonde, blue-eyed, and attractive. I'd expressed an interest in her at one time maybe a year and a half or so ago. She'd made it very clear she wasn't the least bit interested.

"So, you were at Cheaters in the hopes of seeing this woman named Darcy?" Aaron said.

"Yeah, that was one of her names. I also knew her as Cherri."

"From the escort site."

"Yeah, Night Kandy," I said. I didn't want to bring Farrell Finley's name into this, right now, he had enough trouble in his life just trying to get his wife to stay with him. At the mention of Night Kandy, Detective Norah Demming closed her eyes for an overly long moment, suggesting either she couldn't believe it, she wasn't surprised, or maybe both.

"And she'd told you she hung out at Cheaters?"

"Well, umm, no, actually, I spoke to another woman I knew from umm, the Night Kandy site."

"And her name?"

"Chastity."

"Chastity?"

"Yeah, she told me Cherri or Darcy hung out there, I mean at Cheaters, from time to time."

"And you have no idea how the two individuals located you in the parking lot?"

"I can't say for sure, but I have a strong suspicion Darcy spotted me just as soon as she came in the door. She played it cool, and rather than run out of Cheaters, she headed for the ladies' room, where she probably called those two French guys, and then I apparently played into their hands by pulling my car to a dark corner in the back of the lot and sat there waiting."

"Because you were planning to follow them?"

"Yeah, something like that, and before you go any further, yes, I realize now how absolutely stupid that was. I should have called the police. I didn't do that. It was dumb. Guilty as charged."

The door suddenly opened, and Manning hurried in. He shot a disgusted look in my direction and shook his head. As Aaron turned to face him, Manning plastered on a fake smile, then bent over and whispered something to Aaron as he handed him a pink phone message slip.

"Are you kidding me?" Aaron said.

"No, sir. Said he'd like you to contact him just as soon as possible. The number's on the slip. I hung up with him just a minute ago. He's waiting for his connecting flight."

"Okay." Aaron turned back to face me, shaking his head and said, "Something's just come up. I've got to make a phone call. Shouldn't be more than a minute or two, so just hang tight. You need anything?"

"Yeah, umm, Detective Manning, could I get a coffee from you? Black would be just fine."

Manning gave me a look as Aaron got up from his chair and hurried out of the room. "Sure thing, Mr. Haskell. I'd be only too glad to help. Anything else you'd like?"

Norah Demming's back was to Manning. She closed her eyes, smiled, and tried not to laugh. She seemed to be biting her lip.

"No, nothing else. Black coffee would be just fine, thanks."

Forty-seven

Aaron reentered the interview room about five minutes later, shaking his head. "You're never going to believe who I just talked to on the phone."

"Angelina Jolie?"

He shot me a look.

"Okay, you're probably right. I give up."

"Does the name Darcel Renard, Darcy, ring a bell?"

"You just talked to her? She left you her phone number?"

"No. I just spoke with him. *He* called and left me *his* phone number. He's about to board a plane at JFK in New York. He'll be landing here in about three hours."

"He? There's a guy with the same name?"

"Actually, whoever that woman was who conned the two of us, she used his name. Said she was from the Musée d'Orsay in Paris, the same place where this guy heads up the Department of Impressionist Acquisitions, for real, and we bought her bullshit hook, line, and sinker."

"But she was running all those tests. We watched her. She determined that all that canvas was a hundred and twenty-five years old and really rare. She said it was worth a half-million dollars. She—"

"She conned us, Dev, played us for suckers. Yeah, that's what she said. She told us she was running a test with that eyedropper. But it could have been Kool-Aid she put on that canvas, and neither one of us would have known the difference. Jesus Christ."

"But, she was talking to the museum back in Paris at my place. At least that was who she said it was. I was cooking us dinner and—"

"What time was this?"

"Time? I don't know, maybe eight, maybe just a little after."

"And she's calling Paris?"

"Yeah, she was talking French. Said she was talking to someone at the museum. Kind of bitched about people on staff not making a decision while she was gone and that they just—"

"Christ, why the hell didn't I catch it when you first mentioned it? Paris, Dev. They're seven hours ahead of us over there. She's talking to someone in Paris at three in the morning Paris time? Someone from the museum? She was probably passing on the information to those two guys right in front of you, but since neither one of us speaks French and we're too God damned stupid to—"

"Speak for yourself."

"…catch on to the fact that—"

"So, this guy is coming in this afternoon?"

"Yes, and he didn't sound too happy."

"Where are those paintings? The ones with the forgeries covered by that splatter stuff."

"They're all cataloged, and sitting on a shelf down in the evidence room. The guy coming in, the real Darcy, I guess, he wants to examine them and give us the lowdown. I'm going to try and see if he'll view the body."

"The skinny guy, from the trunk of the Mercedes?"

"Yeah, there's an outside chance this guy may know who he is. We did an online search on the fingerprints, but I'm not aware of any results."

"Are we done here?" I asked.

"We are for the moment. You available this afternoon? I might need some reinforcement," Aaron said and shook his head.

"Yeah, but you'll have to contact me personally. My cellphone was in the car when they grabbed me last night, and, well, I don't know where my damn car is."

Aaron looked over at Norah Demming and said, "Can you do a check and see if his vehicle has been located? Dev, what's the license number?"

I had to think for a moment, then came up with a couple of options. It's either DMH 789 or 897 or maybe 978, I'm not sure on the numbers, but the letter prefix is correct. It's a 2007 Dodge Caliber. Sunset Orange Pearl is the color."

"Which has faded to a shitty-looking pink," Aaron said. "You free to give him a lift home?"

"Him? Haskell?" Demming said, looking like she was thinking, *You've got to be kidding.*

"Thanks, Detective. I owe you," Aaron said and walked out of the room.

"You know, I think I invited you over one time, but you were busy, I believe you told me you were going to watch paint dry, or something. So you've never really seen my place, have you? I'll give you a tour and maybe we—"

"Don't even think about it," she said. "You're getting a ride home only because I've been ordered to do it. Believe me, that is the only reason. Period."

Forty-eight

I was seated in the back of a squad car, talking to Detective Demming through the wire mesh screen. I was locked in, and there weren't any door handles on the inside of the back seat. "You sure I can't talk you into a cup of coffee?"

Demming was driving a squad car. We were maybe halfway to my place. I had the feeling she'd grabbed it on purpose rather than her own car or some unmarked vehicle, then made me sit in back instead of the passenger seat, delivering a message that said something like, "Stay the hell away from me."

She glanced at me in the rearview mirror, half laughed, and shook her head. "Unbelievable. Do you ever listen? I told you before. I'm not falling for your bullshit. You bring that up again and I'm going to pull over, kick you out, and you can just walk the rest of the way home."

"Hey, sorry if I was just trying to be nice." I was quiet for a minute, then said, "You like dogs? I got a Golden Retriever. His name is Morton. He'd really like you. He likes ladies."

"I'm sure he does, and no, I'm not going to meet your dog. How old is he?"

"I think he's maybe four or five."

"You don't know?"

"Not really. I rescued him."

"You? You're kidding?"

"No, really."

"Oh, that's sweet."

Aha! "Yeah, someone I knew had him, and well, he wasn't being abused, but he wasn't exactly being taken care of either. This person had him driven damn near neurotic. The poor guy was actually in therapy sessions."

"You're kidding?"

"No, really. I came home one night and there he was, tied to the doorknob with his basket and food dish. I took him in, and we've been pals ever since. He's calmed down quite a bit since then. Actually saved my life once."

"What?"

"Yeah. I had a gig providing security for another dog at a big fancy competition that lasted three days. Thing was named Princess Anastasia, the dog, that is. This was a couple of years back."

"I think I remember that. Wasn't there a shooting or something? It sounded really crazy."

"Yeah, this wacko guy kidnapped her, Princess Anastasia, and tried to sneak out of the Xcel Center with her. It sounds crazy, but there was all sorts of high buck betting going on over what dog would win best of show in the competition, and someone just got carried away, if you'll pardon the pun."

"Unfortunately, it doesn't sound crazy at all. I've been in this line of work long enough to know that there's a certain part of the population that are just plain nuts." She pulled to the curb in front of my place. She studied my house for a long moment. "Hmm-mmm, you live here? It's nice-looking," she said, sounding surprised. Then she climbed out of the squad car and opened the door for me.

As I got out, I saw Morton standing on the couch in the living room. He watched for a moment, then started barking and shaking his head. At the sound of him barking, Demming turned and looked, then said, "Oh, is that him?"

"Yeah, probably needs to be let out. Hi, Morton, hello boy," I said and waved.

"Oh, he's darling."

"You sure you don't want to meet him?"

"Thanks, but I better . . . Well, maybe just for a minute. I love dogs. Unfortunately, it's against the association rules in my condo building, but I love them," she said, then hurried up to the front porch ahead of me.

I opened the front door, and Morton hurried into the entryway, hopped back and forth a couple of times, and then just stood there with his tail wagging. "Hey, Morton, meet Detective Demming. Detective, this is Morton."

"Well, hello, Morton. Oh, you are such a gorgeous boy," she said just as Morton rammed his nose between her legs. "Oh, gee, I wonder who he learned that from?"

I just shrugged and said, "Come on, Morton, let's go outside. You sure I can't make you a cup of coffee?"

"You going to have one?"

"Yeah, I'm putting some on. It'll only take a couple of minutes, and you can get back to trying to find my car. Hey, thanks for the lift home."

"Yeah, hopefully, your car will turn up."

"Aaron was saying it's probably no more than a half-mile from where those guys grabbed me."

"Cheaters," she said, sounding disgusted.

"Yeah, so I hope he was right."

I put the coffee on, chatted with Demming for a few minutes before she hurried out the door. Neither one of us had finished half the coffee in our mug, but at least I'd gotten her inside, and she hadn't pulled her weapon on me, so I considered it a win.

Forty-nine

Aaron rang my doorbell a little after four. "Oh, good, hoping I'd catch you home."

"Where was I going to go, remember? I'm without a set of wheels."

"Mind if I bring the world's most unhappy guy from Paris in?"

I glanced over his shoulder at the unmarked car in front of my house. I could feel the tension as the guy in the passenger seat turned, looked at me, and then plastered a disgusted frown on his face.

"Whoa, that's one unhappy camper."

"I can't really blame him."

"Yeah, bring him in. Think he'd like some coffee?"

Aaron's back was to me. He was waving his arm in an attempt to signal his passenger to come in. If the guy noticed, you sure couldn't tell. Finally, Aaron stepped off the front porch. The guy turned and faced him when he was about two steps away from the car, frowned, then climbed out of the passenger seat.

"Dev," Aaron said, climbing back onto the porch. "I'd like you to meet Monsieur Darcel Renard from the Musée d'Orsay in Paris."

"Pleased to meet you, Monsieur Renard," I said and extended my hand. He seemed to grudgingly take it, but really didn't squeeze back as I shook his hand. "Please, please, come on in," I said, then held the door for them.

"Dev," Aaron said, "Monsieur Renard has just flown in from Paris to examine the forgeries we acquired. I'd like to show him the canvases that were left behind here."

"Yeah, sure, I've got them up in the guest room. Come on," I said and led the way up the stairs. "I checked them all earlier this morning after you dropped me off. They're all empty. I mean, there's nothing underneath the splatter canvas. I'm guessing he had these just sitting around, and then once he finished another forgery, he would pull off one of these canvases and tack it over the forgery." I opened the door to my guest room and extended my hand to the two of them. Aaron stepped into the room then moved to the side so Renard could get to the stack of canvases leaning against the far wall.

He frowned as he approached and picked one of them up. The lower left-hand corner of the canvas where I had pulled the staples flapped as he lifted the painting. He held the canvas at arm's length, shook his head disgustedly, then looked at the two of us and said, "You think this is absolute shit. No?"

"Absolutely. Shit. I mean, yes," Aaron said.

"As you can see, they're all like that," I said.

He pulled a small magnifying glass from his pocket and examined the corner of the painting, then stuck his bottom lip out, nodded, and said, "Actually, despite what you think, this is quite good."

"Good?" Aaron and I said together.

Renard nodded.

"That splatter shit? Any five-year-old child could do that in about five minutes," I said.

"I think not," Renard said, flashing a cold smile then turned to Aaron. "I should next like to see the work you have arrested."

"Yeah, okay, sure, they're being held down at our station, in the evidence room. Tightly secured," Aaron said.

"Really?" Renard said, sounding doubtful regarding local police capabilities.

"Dev, you want to come with? You can check on your vehicle while you're down there."

"Yeah, let me just lock up the back, and I'll join you." I hurried to the back, called Morton in, then locked the door and went out the front. I climbed into the backseat of the car, and Aaron took off toward downtown and the main station.

On the way to the station, we stopped at a red light. A guy with a homeless sign began to approach the car, but then backed off when Renard shot him a look. Actually, I knew the guy. His name was Billy, and any problems he had were more or less self-inflicted with the help of about a fifth of vodka per day. I waved from the backseat once the light changed, and we pulled away.

Fifty

It took some time while the keeper of the gate in the evidence room scanned Renard's French passport. Aaron had to vouch for him and get signatures from superiors two levels up before Renard had permission to remove the splatter canvas from one of the forgeries underneath. Aaron told him to pick whichever one he wanted to take a look at, and then the two of us stepped back and let him go to work.

Renard opened his briefcase, took out a large linen-looking sheet, and placed it over the table in the conference room. He pulled on a white lab coat, a pair of white cotton gloves and what looked like a surgical mask. It took him a good twenty minutes to meticulously remove the staples around the splatter canvas, which he then carefully placed on the far end of the table. He stepped back and examined the forgery on the table before him, folding his arms and nodding. He was now in his own little world, oblivious to the two of us standing off in a corner.

The painting was of a naked woman sitting on a white towel with a fringe on the end. Instead of facing the artist, she was staring away with her left arm resting between her knees. She had long auburn hair down to the middle of her back, and she looked like she could have been seventeen or eighteen. She had a smirk on her face, maybe. The background did not appear to have the same attention to detail as the figure of the woman.

After a number of minutes, Renard looked up at Aaron and me and said, "Young girl Bathing. Pierre Auguste Renoir, 1892." He took out a magnifying glass and attached it to his eyeglasses, just in front of the lens on the right side, then snapped the magnifying glass over the lens and bent over the painting. He remained in that position for a good ten minutes, not saying anything, occasionally shaking his head. He studied the lower left-hand corner for another five minutes, then stepped back, removed a camera from his briefcase, and proceeded to take close to two dozen pictures, at least a half dozen of which were of the lower corner.

When he'd finished, he stepped back, set the camera down, and flicked the magnifying lens up from his glasses before he turned to look at us.

"What do you think?" Aaron asked.

Renard pursed his lips, apparently thinking for a long moment, then said, "The thin brush strokes, the colors, the signature and date in the left-hand corner, the apparent speed by which the background is completed, as if by memory. Just exactly the way Renoir worked. Remarkable. Nothing short of genius. I have no idea how he did this without actually having the work in front of him, and even then, most impossible."

"So, even though it's a forgery, it's good," Aaron said.

"No, it's not good. It is excellent. Easily the best I've ever seen. I would like to contact my office and tell them I'm extending my stay. I'll need to examine all the paintings. Additionally, this work, the splatter, as you referred to it."

"Yeah, that kiddy art shit," I said.

Renard stared at me for a long moment, then said, "I'm not an expert, but my first glance suggests the American expressionist artist Jackson Pollock. This would appear to be a copy, although at a different size, of his work entitled Number 5, 1948."

"That's the name of the thing, 1948?"

"Number 5, 1948," he corrected. "Before you prove my suspicions further, I'd remind you that the original was reported sold for one hundred and forty million dollars in 2006. That painting, the original, was actually done on fiberboard, but still, this is most impressive. I should like to meet the gentleman who created these works. They may be forgeries, but as I said, they are certainly of a quality the like of which I've never seen before."

"Yeah," Aaron said. "We'd like to meet him, too. There is one other thing you might be able to help us with."

"More forgery?"

"Actually, no. To our knowledge, there were three individuals involved in taking these paintings. They all spoke French, although there is some suggestion that at least one of them was from Canada. We do have one of them. Would you have time to take a look at him?"

"More than take a look, I should like to talk to him."

"I'm not sure how well that will work, but we can try. We've got him no more than five minutes away. Shall we go see him?" Aaron asked and smiled.

"Yes, by all means," Renard said, quickly removing his lab coat and then closing his briefcase.

Thirty seconds later, we were headed out the door. Renard was excitedly rattling on nonstop, telling Aaron he was anxious to learn anything he could about the talented forger.

Fifty-one

The Ramsey County Medical Examiner's office was a nondescript, one-story brick building located on lower University Ave. The parking lot consisted of ten spaces, eight of which were used by full-time employees. Fortunately, the remaining two spaces were empty, and Aaron pulled into the first one. Renard either didn't see the sign at the entrance or maybe it didn't translate to whatever the French word is for "morgue."

"You have him here?" he said as he got out of the front passenger seat.

"Yes, he's just inside," Aaron said and headed for the door.

Inside, the reception area featured a faux leather couch and two matching chairs, a glass-topped coffee table, and a white plastic stand in the corner, which held a number of different brochures touting cremation services. A receptionist's desk was positioned behind a large glass panel in the wall.

A dark-haired woman who looked to be in her late twenties was seated at the receptionist desk, and as Aaron approached, she looked up and said, "Hi, Lieutenant."

"How's it going Carol?"

"Different day, same, uhh, activity," she said, then smiled at Renard and me. "What can I do for you?"

"Like to view the John Doe placed here yesterday. We have a gentleman who has come all the way over from Paris."

"Oh, really," she said, then seemed to catch Renard's eye and said, "Bienvenue à Saint Paul."

Renard smiled, said something back in French, then looked the other way to bring an end to the conversation.

Carol rolled her eyes, then said, "Let me get someone to escort you back to the viewing room." She picked up the phone, pressed three keys, and waited for a long moment. "Yeah, Wally, I've got Lieutenant LaZelle out here with two individuals to view the John Doe from yesterday. Yeah, okay. Thanks," she said and hung up. "Wally will be out here in just a moment. He's just in the process of finishing something up."

I took the 'finishing something up' comment to mean whoever Wally was, he was probably involved in an autopsy. Sure enough, the security door to the rest of the facility opened about five minutes later, and a bald guy in blue scrubs said, "Hey, Lieutenant, you got a name for us?"

"We'll find out in a moment, Doc," Aaron said.

Renard and I followed them down the hall. Renard was getting a strange look on his face the further down the hall we went. Wally held a door open for us with the brass number three attached to the door, and we stepped inside.

"Be just a minute, and I'll wheel him up," Wally said, then pulled the door closed behind us.

The room was small, painted off-white, with grey carpet. It was devoid of any furniture and had a picture window in one wall. Blinds on the far side of the window were drawn closed.

Renard gave Aaron a questioning look and said, "Will we be able to talk to him, this man, this Mr. Doe?"

"Probably not," Aaron said, keeping a straight face.

A minute later, the blinds were raised, and there was Wally standing at one end of the trolley wheeled up in front of the window. A white cloth covered the entire trolley. If you knew what lay beneath the cloth, you could just make out the outline of a body beneath the cloth.

Renard shot a surprised look at Aaron. Aaron nodded at Wally, who then carefully stepped forward, lifted the cloth and folded it back beneath the thin guy's chin. He tugged the edges of the cloth so that it was snug up against the guy's neck.

He was definitely dead, although he'd been cleaned up since I last saw him in the trunk of the Mercedes. The blood was gone from the side of his head and his face.

The bruises and cuts from my belt buckle were still visible, but nowhere near as vicious-looking as the last time I'd seen him. The bullet hole above the right eye was barely the size of a dime and appeared more puckered than an open hole. The eyelids were at half-mast, but beneath them, you could just make out a pair of glassy brown eyes.

Renard's eyes were wide, and he stared for a long moment, then shook his head and said, "Pascal. It is Pascal Bouchard."

"You're sure?" Aaron said.

"Yes, yes. It's him. He's well known. Has quite the reputation," Renard said, then shook his head again. "But to end up like this, here. It is the waste. No?"

"Yes, a real waste," Aaron said. "I would like you to fill out a small form for our records if you wouldn't mind."

"Yes, yes, but of course," Darcel said in almost a whisper. Then he cleared his throat and shook his head. "Oh, Pascal, such a waste of your talent. He was a top student and was on our staff for a short while, perhaps twenty years ago. Somewhere he took the wrong turn. A shame, so sad, oh, quel dommage."

Aaron gave Wally a nod, then extended his hand toward the door so Darcel would be the first to leave. Wally closed the blinds just as Darcel hurried out of the room.

Fifty-two

We were sipping coffee in Aaron's office, Aaron, myself, and Darcel Renard. Darcel actually began to exhibit a bit of a personality and, in between yawns, was entertaining us with stories of Pascal Bouchard. It turned out Pascal had paired up with a wayward uncle, Maynor Bouchard, and entered the business of art theft and forgery, which up until last night had apparently treated them rather well.

"Oh, they made the money and a lot of it. Very private, the two of them, careful to always live the quiet life. How do I say? They were well known, always suspected, but never actually caught in the act. You know, perhaps this sort?"

Aaron nodded that yes, he did indeed know the sort. "And the woman? Did they have a woman accomplice?" Aaron asked.

Darcel seemed to think for a long moment, gradually shaking his head, then finally he looked up and said, "No, to what I know, I've never heard of it. Perhaps she was going to replace Maynor, although I'm not aware of such an act. But he must be seventy years, now, Maynor. Maybe they were going to make her a partner. I would say based on the result I saw this afternoon, Pascal, dead, she would no longer be welcome. Now, I must apologize, but it is sleep that I need, and then back tomorrow to continue my examination of the paintings you have. Could someone bring me to my hotel?"

Aaron nodded, then picked up the phone and made an internal call. A moment later, two guys were at the office door. We walked Darcel to the elevator, said our goodbyes, and then a very tired-looking Darcel Renard, the real one, headed off to his hotel.

"I suppose you need a lift home," Aaron said to me once the elevator doors had closed.

"Yeah, if you wouldn't mind."

"Actually, I do mind, but I'll give you a lift anyway. Come on, I'm dragging, let's get the hell out of here. It's been an awfully long day."

"At least Colleen Lacy is okay. God, I wonder where in the hell Demarcus is?"

"If he has any brains, he's nowhere around this town," Aaron said. "I'm thinking there's a very strong possibility he's our shooter. The two, Maynor and Pascal, uncle and nephew together for twenty or thirty years, and then one shoots the other? I guess it's possible, but there's a greater chance your pal is our shooter."

"God, Demarcus, it just doesn't make sense."

"Aren't you the guy basically fingered him for forging museum-quality impressionist paintings?"

"Yeah, right. I know, I know," I said in response to the look I got.

Aaron shut down his office, talked to someone on the way out for a couple of minutes before we headed to the parking lot. I climbed in the front seat, and he took off for my place. We were halfway there before I broke the silence. "You know, I've been thinking—"

"Oh shit," Aaron suddenly said and glanced over at me. He rolled his eyes and reached into his pocket. "Not you, Dev, it's my damn cell. Yeah, hello. What? You're kidding, where? Damage? Okay, on my way. Thanks, appreciate the call. Be there in about ten minutes, just hang tight," he said, then hung up and accelerated.

"Everything okay?"

"As we speak, one of our squads is standing guard over a faded pink 2007 Dodge Caliber."

"Is it mine?"

"No, Dev, there's someone else in town with an exact replica of your horse shit car. You kidding? Yes, it's yours. It's parked in front of a driveway, and by the way, not too far from Cheaters. I knew it."

"God, I hope it still runs."

"I'm sure whoever stole it probably just wanted to get it tuned up, change the oil and top off everything for you."

We were there in about six minutes. A squad car was parked directly behind my car. Two cops were leaning against the hood of the squad car, talking to a nice-looking woman. As we pulled up behind, and I hopped out, one of them said, "Oh, here they are now."

I hurried to the car and opened the driver's door. The keys were gone from the ignition. I quickly checked the floor and the seat but didn't see them anywhere. "Shit," I said.

"Looking for these?" one of the cops said, dangling my keys out in front of him.

"This wouldn't happen to be yours too, would it?" the other cop asked and held out my cellphone.

"Oh, man, you guys are great," I said, then glanced at my cell. It looked like someone had stepped on the screen. The glass was still in place, but it was all cracked. The cop handed me the phone, and I pushed a button. The screen immediately lit up, and the thing apparently still worked.

"Looks like some artist took your car," the other cop said as he handed the keys to me.

"Huh?" I said, then looked at the driver's side. Someone had spray-painted a quick sketch of a person bending over. The image was positioned so that the gas cap was right where the butt would be. Both cops started chuckling. I walked around to the passenger side, and there in black spray paint, someone had written, "Sorry about your car." There was a parking ticket beneath the windshield wiper, and I pulled it off and headed toward the cops.

"Did you guys do this?" I asked and waved the ticket.

Everyone laughed, the two cops, Aaron, and the woman.

"Wish we'd thought of it, but no way, man. That's from our friends in Parking Enforcement," one of the cops said.

"Better see if it starts," Aaron suggested.

I hopped in, turned the key in the ignition, and the car started up on the second try. It sounded about the same as it usually did, and I shut it off.

"Thing doesn't sound all that great," the woman said as I slid out of the car. A dark cloud of exhaust fumes was just beginning to dissipate.

"Hey, you got your car back. You can file a protest on the ticket tomorrow. You're good to go home, plus you got your phone, and it still works. I think you should maybe just consider yourself lucky," Aaron said.

I shook hands with the cops, thanked them for the call to Aaron. I apologized to the woman for my stolen car being left blocking her driveway, and I thanked Aaron for the lift, then got back in my graffiti-adorned car and drove home.

Fifty-three

I'd only been home for a minute and had just let Morton out into the backyard when my cellphone rang.

"Hello?" I said after carefully swiping my finger across the shattered cellphone screen.

"Dude, it's about damn time. Where in the hell have you been, man? Didn't you get any of my messages?" Farrell Finley.

"Hey, Farrell. Messages? No, sorry, I just got my phone back not more than twenty minutes ago. Some bastard stole my car from the parking lot at Cheaters."

"Well, I can use some advice, if not some help."

"What's up?"

"I got a call from Cherri. She sounded desperate. Actually, she sounded way worse than desperate. She sounded scared to death."

"What? She called you? You actually talked to her? Please tell me you're not kidding."

"Yeah, we talked, but for no more than half a minute. No one was more surprised than me. She wanted the two of us to come and get her. Said she was ready to turn herself in but needed protection."

"Protection? What the hell was she talking about?"

"I don't know, man. I mean, she wouldn't say. We only talked for like thirty seconds."

"What'd you tell her?"

"God, I couldn't just leave her hanging. I mean she was crying on the phone, begging me. I'm not too good when it comes to chicks crying, dude. I'm supposed to meet her at ten."

That was twenty minutes from now. "Where is she?"

"She wouldn't tell me, just said she'd meet me at Cheaters at ten."

Cheaters. The more I thought about it, in a strange way, it made sense. Darcy, or Cherri, or whatever her name was, was a fairly attractive woman. There'd be a dozen guys jumping to her defense if someone hassled her.

"Dev, you there, man?"

"Yeah. Listen, you sure it was her?"

"Pretty sure. I mean she, ahh, called me, you know, by my sign-in name from the escort site."

"What was that?"

"Ummm, Stud Muffin One," he said after a long pause.

"Oh, yeah, how could I forget. Okay, I can get there, to Cheaters, but I gotta leave now. See you there, Farrell. Let's meet in the parking lot," I said, then hung up and hurried out the door. I thought about calling Aaron on my way there, but then decided against it, squad cars might scare her away. I figured once we had her in our custody we could call the cops. That way, if Farrell didn't want to be involved, he could leave before the cops even showed up.

I had parked in Cheaters' parking lot and was just getting out of my car when a red F150 drove alongside the building and headed into an open space about a half-dozen down from me. Farrell.

"Hey, man," he called as he climbed out of his truck. "Thanks for coming. God, she sounded like she was really frightened. Said she'd do anything for us if we gave her protection." I must have given Farrell a look. "Relax, dude, that's really the last thing I need in my life right now. Still, I couldn't just leave her hanging. I brought some firepower," he said and pulled what looked like a deer rifle out from behind the driver's seat.

"Hey, Farrell, put that damn thing away before someone calls the cops on us. Let's go inside and see what the hell is scaring her. You know I'm going to want to get the cops involved."

"Yeah, fine with me. Tell you the truth, the way she sounded, I think that'll probably be fine with her, too. Might be why she wanted your ass involved. She's convinced she needs some heavy-duty protection."

I tucked my pistol into the small of my back, pulled my shirt out to cover it, and we headed into Cheaters. The place was crowded, all the tables were filled, and guys were standing along the edge of the area just behind the tables. Everyone was focused on the stage where two women were showing off their exemplary skills, twirling round and round on a brass pole. I looked around but didn't see anyone resembling Darcy. I checked the back corner of the bar. There were a half-dozen women seated back there. Three or four of them wore a pasted-on longing look and stared at me. One ran her tongue slowly across her upper lip, and another wiggled her index finger, beckoning me forward. I headed over to the woman wiggling her finger.

"Looking to party, baby?" she said, then turned on her barstool and faced me in a pose that placed her figure on full display.

"Actually, no. I was supposed to meet someone here. She goes by Cherri, sometimes, said she'd meet me here at ten. You know her?"

"I might," she said, turning back toward the bar and leaning forward on her elbows. "It'll cost you, though."

I figured if Darcy/Cherri had told this woman anything, she wouldn't be playing the money game now, so I looked her up and down, then said, "No thanks."

She just frowned, shook her head, and turned her back to me.

I did see the waitress I'd talked to the other night. She was dressed in another French maid outfit, only this one seemed to fit much better, and in fact might have been a size or two too small. It didn't appear to be torn anywhere. Tonight her hair was in a single braid that hung down to the middle of her back, and the bags that had been under her eyes the other night had all but disappeared. She appeared more or less put together.

I walked over to her, waited while she delivered an order of beers to a table, then stepped toward her just as she turned in my direction. "Hi. Remember me?"

"God, do I owe you money or something?"

"No, no, nothing like that. I asked you about a woman the other night, had a Canadian hockey tattoo on her lower back."

"Oh, sorry, yeah, now I remember. Of course, that tattoo, right above her ass, right? She danced here a couple of times."

"Yeah, that's the one. She was going to meet me and my pal here. Did you happen to see her around tonight?" I said, then pulled a twenty from my wallet and held it between my thumb and forefinger.

She stared at the cash for a half-second, then shook her head no and looked disappointed. "No, sorry, I ain't seen her."

I tossed the twenty on her empty tray and said, "Could you do me a favor and just check the ladies' room and the dressing room and see if she's in there? You don't have to say anything to her, just let me know."

"And you're not a cop?"

"No. She called my friend," I pointed toward Farrell, still scanning the room. "Wanted both of us here tonight."

"God," she said, sizing up Farrell. "She's sure gonna earn her money tonight. Okay, give me just a second, and I'll be right back." She hurried past a number of tables toward the far side of the room then around a corner. She was heading back to me three minutes later, shaking her head as she approached.

"Hey, sorry, unless she's that really drunk chick throwing up in the can she's not in there or in the dressing room."

"Did you check the woman throwing up? Did you actually see her?"

"Relax. She's Asian. She's not who you're looking for."

"Okay, thanks," I said and headed back over to Farrell. He'd been scanning the room the entire time.

"You see anything?"

"A couple of guys from my neighborhood, they pretended they didn't know me. I didn't see anyone that looks like Cherri."

"Yeah, I just had someone check the can and the dressing room, she's not in there. You want to wait in here for a bit? I'll buy you a beer."

Farrell seemed to think about that for a brief second, then nodded yes. I bought a round of beers, then Farrell bought a round after that. By the time we'd finished the second round, Darcy still hadn't shown.

"Your call. What do ya think?" I said. It was a little after eleven.

Farrell gave another quick scan around the room, then shook his head. "I'm not seeing her. You'd think she would have been watching for us to show up. It sure as hell don't look like she's here. Sorry, Dev, guess I got us on a wild goose chase. Might as well take off, if she hasn't shown up by now I don't think we're gonna see her. Besides, my kids got dance lessons at nine tomorrow morning, and it's my week to take 'em. I'm thinking we might as well head out."

We both gave the place one more final look around, but couldn't spot her. The waitress I'd given the twenty to gave me a little wave, and the woman who wiggled her finger to get me to come over when we'd first arrived gave me her middle finger then turned on her stool so she wouldn't have to look at me.

Once outside, the parking lot seemed to have thinned out ever so slightly. I immediately looked to where I'd parked and felt a sense of relief when I spotted my car. I could just make out the spray-painted figure strategically positioned around my gas cap.

"I don't get it, man. She sounded so desperate on the phone. I mean, the chick was begging."

"Who knows, Farrell. Sometimes they can—"

"Hey, you hear that?" Farrell said.

"Is that thumping?"

"Yeah, and someone yelling. It's coming from over by my truck," he said and started moving two rows over, picking up speed as he went.

Fifty-four

Farrell was four cars ahead of me, moving fast and winding his way around parked cars like they were linemen trying to tackle him. He was headed toward a dark-colored car with a red convertible top. As I got closer, I saw the car was a blue BMW, exactly like the one I'd shot the rear tires on just last night.

By the time I caught up, Farrell was standing at the rear of the car, knocking on the trunk. "Hello, hello."

"Oh, help, help, get me out of here. Please, help me, I beg." I picked up on the French accent.

"Cherri?" Farrell said, then looked at me and nodded.

"Oh, yes, yes, is that you? Muffin?"

"Yeah, Stud Muffin One. I got Dev Haskell with me. You just hang on there, Cheri. I'll get you out of there in just a minute."

"Hurry, hurry. Please, there is not much time."

Farrell went over and tried the driver's door. It was locked. He hurried around to the passenger side and tried that door. Also locked. He seemed to swear under his breath, went back to the driver's door, half-turned, and sent an elbow crashing through the window. The alarm on the BMW sounded, and he opened the door, then reached down, pulled a lever, and the trunk popped no more than an inch. He stepped to the rear, lifted the lid, and I could hear what sounded like crying coming from the trunk.

"Come on, come on, there. You're all right. Give me your hand, Cherri. Yeah, that's right, watch your head. Come on, that's right, that's right. You're okay. It's okay, you're out of there. You're gonna be okay."

He half-lifted her out of the car. She buried her head against his chest and continued sobbing. He wrapped his arms around her, then signaled me with a wave of his head.

"Hey, Dev, you better check this out."

I came around the back of the car and looked into the trunk. Farrell still had his arms wrapped around her, not in a romantic sort of way, but rather as protection. I peered into the trunk of the BMW. There was a grimy dark wool blanket covering a large mass of something, and then in the far corner of the trunk, where the blanket had been pulled away, what looked an awful lot like a forehead peeked out from beneath the blanket.

The bald head and the bad dye job on the fringe of hair looked familiar. I lifted the blanket ever so slightly, exposing a big nose and swarthy skin. Fatty. Maynor Bouchard. Wayward uncle to Pascal Bouchard, and with a bullet hole in his forehead to match.

I looked at Farrell and said, "Not good. I'm calling the cops."

Farrell nodded and seemed to wrap his arms around the sobbing woman just that much tighter.

I stepped to the driver's door, looked inside beneath the dash, and pulled a lever that popped the hood open. I went to the front of the car, pushed a lever that released the secondary lock, then raised the hood support and spotted the car horn, continuing to sound the alarm. I pulled some wires leading into the horn, but the noise continued. Then I spotted a cable running from the bottom of the device, yanked on it a couple of times, and suddenly an eerie silence settled into Cheaters' parking lot. The only thing I heard was my ears ringing.

I pulled my cellphone out, and suddenly a voice from two cars over shouted, "Please don't do that, Dev."

I looked up, and Demarcus was coming toward us, waving a pistol first at me and then at Farrell.

"Just move back by your pal."

"Demarcus, what the hell are you—"

"Hey, did you hear me? I said, move over by your pal and Cherri."

I raised my hands and walked back by Farrell. "Demarcus, I don't know what you got planned, but it's not going to work. You better just get your ass the hell out of here before the cops get you."

Three guys suddenly stepped around the corner of the building. "Did you check her out? You could see she had the hots for me. I'm telling you, she really—"

"What the hell?" one of them said as all three stopped at the same time and stared at Demarcus holding the pistol and me with my hands still up.

"Get the fuck out of here," Demarcus yelled.

They remained glued to the spot, staring at us.

"Did you hear what I just said? Get your ass out of here."

The three of them took off running back around the corner of the building.

"God damn it," he said, approaching, and waving the pistol at us. "You just couldn't leave well enough alone, had to get involved. Didn't you? I needed one more day, but you had to stick your nose in. And you, you stupid bitch."

Farrell seemed to swallow, audibly, then moved Cherri behind him with a meaty arm and leveled his gaze at Demarcus.

"Oh yeah, that's right, the whore's hero. It didn't have to be this way. One more day and I would have been set for life. All that time, effort, years of study, and you guys fucked it all up for me. Your idea of art, Dev, is a coloring book," he said.

We suddenly heard a siren in the distance.

"Shit," Demarcus said. "Sorry, man, but you've left me no other option. Well, ladies first, bitch," he said, then pointed his pistol at Cherri peeking out from behind Farrell.

My shot was loud, followed by two more. Demarcus took a step back, got a surprised look on his face, then grabbed his throat with both hands just as blood started to run out of his mouth.

Cherri screamed.

Demarcus dropped to the ground, and I hurried past Farrell wrapping his arm around Cherri so she wouldn't see Demarcus twitching on the ground. He was on his back, both hands still around his throat. His legs moved like he was trying to run, feet scraping against the pavement.

As I approached, I aimed at his chest, kicked his pistol to the side, then knelt down next to him. Blood was pooling around his head and shoulders, and he gurgled something as if he was trying to speak. He stared at me with a questioning look for just a second or two before his eyes took on a glassy, distant stare. He twitched once or twice and then remained still.

"You dumb, stupid, son of a bitch," I screamed. "What did you think you were doing, Demarcus? What the hell did you think you were going to do? Demarcus. Answer me. Demarcus."

Fifty-five

Aaron had arrived about twenty minutes after the first squad. That was well over an hour ago. Now there were a half-dozen squad cars. An ambulance had Cherri on a gurney in the back with an oxygen mask over her face. A BCA van was parked near the back of the BMW. Two guys in white hazmat suits were going over the trunk of the car with a fine-toothed comb. Maynor Bouchard had been pulled from the trunk and was resting in a black body bag on a gurney next to the car. A fairly large area had been taped off all around the car. Demarcus was still on the ground, but white nylon screens had been set up to hide his body from the curious. Two guys in hazmat suits were in the process of taking his fingerprints.

If this were anywhere else, there would have been a crowd of people watching. I found it interesting that patrons leaving Cheaters gave a curious look, grew suddenly wide-eyed once they had an inkling of what had occurred, then seemed to quickly decide they didn't want to be anywhere near, hurried into their cars and drove off. Two guys, obviously over-served, had the foresight to pocket their car keys, leave their car in the lot, then turn on their heels and walk home rather than risk a DUI from one of the almost dozen cops milling around in the parking lot.

"No," Farrell said to Aaron for the umpteenth time. "She called me and said she wanted to meet me here at ten. Me and Dev. I figured she meant inside. She never mentioned anything about the parking lot or her car. I didn't even know that BMW was hers, and I had no idea she was in the trunk until I got to it. We just heard someone calling for help when we came out of Cheaters."

"You didn't recognize the BMW?" Aaron said to me. Detective Manning was standing just behind him, shaking his head.

"I didn't see it until I followed Farrell over. I can't even tell you if it was here when we pulled in. To be honest, I figured you guys would have had it impounded after last night. How'd she or Demarcus even gain access to it?"

"One of the many questions we have," Aaron said and looked at Manning.

A guy in a hazmat suit approached and said, "Lieutenant, there's no identification. You said you've got a tentative ID on the victim?"

Aaron nodded and said, "We suspect he's a French national, although there's an outside chance he might be Canadian. We think the name is Maynor Bouchard, age approximately seventy. I've got someone who will hopefully be able to identify him tomorrow. I'll personally have him over at the medical examiners in the morning.

The woman should also be able to identify him," Aaron said, then indicated the ambulance with Cherri in the back.

"Yeah, unfortunately, they've given her a pretty strong sedative. They'll have to keep her at Regions overnight."

"We'll have someone there making sure she stays the night. I don't want her disappearing."

As Aaron spoke, the guy wrote down Maynor Bouchard's name on a white card, not much bigger than a business card, and it suddenly dawned on me he was writing on a toe tag. When he finished, he nodded and headed back to the gurney with the body bag.

"You going to charge her?" I asked.

"We know she let the two Bouchards into your place. She was probably involved in your abduction, the Colleen Lacy kidnapping, possession of stolen property. She impersonated Darcel Renard, interfered with our ongoing investigation. Much as I'd like to charge her on tonight's activity, it's really not a crime to get locked in the trunk of a car with a body and have someone attempt to shoot you. That said, we've certainly got some rather persuasive arguments we can present to her. So yeah, I'm thinking she's going to be charged, and probably be residing in a secure facility for a number of years, compliments of the great State of Minnesota."

"Hey, Lieutenant, if you're finished with me tonight, I'd like to just head home. I wanna hug my kids.

They'll be asleep, but so what. Then I want to hug the wife and just hold her," Farrell said.

Aaron looked over at Detective Manning, who nodded. "Appreciate your help, Mr. Finley," Aaron said. "I'd like you to come down tomorrow morning to give us a formal statement. We can work around your schedule. Just ask for Detective Manning or me."

Manning grudgingly nodded, and you could see Farrell immediately thinking Manning was going to be the last person he asked for.

"Thanks, Dev. Sorry it ended up this way."

"Hey, relax, Farrell. I'm just glad you weren't hurt. It brings a number of things to a close. We'll talk tomorrow. Oh, hey," I called as he began to step away. "Have a nice time at dance class tomorrow."

"Yeah, thanks," he said, then hurried over to the far side of the parking lot, climbed into his pickup truck and drove off.

Aaron talked to a couple of cops for a few minutes, then stepped back over to me. "What do you think?" I asked.

"I'd say she's a lucky lady and got one hell of a wakeup call that crime doesn't pay. This make any sense to you? What was he trying to accomplish?"

"I have no idea what in the hell he was thinking. He seemed so inept, so unorganized, and then, I don't know."

"Yeah, and then it turns out he's been producing the best masterpiece forgeries the guy from Paris has ever seen. And just to make it interesting, he's hidden them under another set of forgeries of an American artist. I have a feeling he's been playing a number of people for quite some time," Aaron said.

"But the guy lived with me, I took him in and then he's all of a sudden going to kill the three of us?"

"I'd say there's a pretty strong chance he just flipped out once all his work was confiscated."

"Well, when you find out, be sure to let me know. Now, if it's okay, I'm going to follow Farrell's lead and head for home, unless there's something else you need to know."

"No, you might as well take off. I'm out of here in the next half-hour. I'll expect you in here sometime tomorrow morning to submit a statement. If I'm not here you can talk to Manning. He'll be only too happy to help."

"You gotta be kidding me. You know how that's going to go down. He'll have me arrested for something or other."

"Dev, just do it, okay."

"All right, all right. God, I'll be happy to do so," I said, not meaning a word. "Keep an eye on our lady friend over there. She seems to be the key right now."

"Gee, really? Thanks for that tip. I never would have figured it out."

Fifty-Six

I called Aaron the following morning, twice, and ended up leaving a message both times. I headed down to the police station around 11:00 to give them my statement and ran into Farrell Finley and his wife in the main lobby.

"Hey, Farrell, did you already give them your statement?"

"Yeah. I had to deal with that Detective Manning character, but he wasn't half-bad. Had some questions about you, but I think I set him straight."

"Questions about me?"

"Yeah, umm." He glanced at his wife for a moment and said, "Honey, this is kind of private information. I wonder if you could just give me a minute with Dev."

She nodded and said, "When you two are finished, I want a minute of your time, too, Dev." Then she stepped outside and lit a cigarette. We watched her take a long first drag and blow a cloud of smoke into the air.

"So, how'd it go?"

"You mean with Manning? Okay, I just maybe put a little different spin on some things."

"Different spin?"

"Hey, come on, my wife was sitting right next to me. You think I wanted her to know I was stupid enough to use the name Stud Muffin One as my sign-in name? You think I want her to know I knew Cherri from before?" Then he added, "Even though nothing ever happened."

"Okay, I guess I can deal with that. Anything else?"

"Well, I think the reason she wants to talk to you is to cancel your investigation of me."

"Cancel it?"

"Dude, I was holding her for most of the night and crying my eyes out. We're going to counseling, starting next Wednesday. I'm trying to put shit back together in our marriage. It would really help if you could, you know, confirm that nothing happened with those escorts."

"Oh, Farrell."

"Come on, man, you talked to both of them, Chastity and Cherri, they told you nothing happened. Even though I ended up having to pay 'em."

"Okay, okay, I get it."

"Oh, and just one more thing."

"Yeah," I said, not too sure where this was going to go.

"I, ahh, told her I was one of them CIA undercover operators."

"CIA? Farrell, come on, man, and by the way, you meant an undercover operative. Right?"

"Yeah, that's the one, I guess. It's why she was down here this morning. I got her buying into it now and, well, it would really help if you could back me up. You know? Besides, I mean, I think you did say I saved Cherri's life."

"Well, yeah, but—"

"Thanks, dude. I owe you. I'm gonna tell her to come in here now. Okay? Just make sure you back me up."

I sighed, then nodded.

"Good. You won't regret it, man," Farrell said and then hurried out of the building. He looked excited as he said something to his wife. She nodded, blew a lung full of smoke up into the clear blue sky, then dropped her cigarette onto the ground and stubbed it out with the toe of her shoe. She turned and came back into the building as Farrell gave me the thumbs-up through the window.

"Hi, Dev. God, I wish you would have told me all this. It sure as hell would have saved me a lot of heartache and sleepless nights."

"Well, yeah, I guess, I probably should have."

"Relax, I get it. I mean top-secret, undercover with the CIA, you can't let on. So anyway, go ahead and drop your investigation of Farrell. I mean, who are we kidding? I don't want to goof up the investigation of the Russians manipulating the art market."

"Yeah, okay. That sounds good, real good. Of course, I won't charge you anything for the time spent."

"Well, yeah, no shit, Sherlock," she half-laughed. "Hey, not to worry, my lips are sealed. Oh, man, we better take off, the kids are finished at dance class in about fifteen minutes. Ummm, I'm going to tell Farrell he has to promise to knock off this undercover shit. We decided to try for number three, and I don't want him doing this anymore. Nothing personal, you know, it's just, well, you know."

"Not to worry, I get it. No offense taken," I said.

"Thanks," she said, then hurried out the door.

I was escorted up to Homicide and asked for Aaron. Unfortunately, he was busy, and I ended up giving my statement to Manning. Surprisingly that went just fine, and I was out of there in an hour. On my way down to the office, my cellphone rang.

"Hello."

"Oh, so you *are* alive," Heidi said.

"Hey, how's it going?"

"Wonderful, if you must know. I'm calling to see if you could join me for dinner tonight. I'm celebrating, and if you behave, there just might be something very special for you."

I liked the sound of that. "Celebrating what? And before you answer, yes, I can join you. You thinking of going out? I've got some great bratwurst I could do on the grill."

"Yeah, Dev, that would be a special celebration, bratwurst on your grill and drinking beer out of the bottle until you have me so drunk I wouldn't remember a thing."

"Sounds like a great night. What's your point?"

"We'll be having a lovely dinner at my place. You can show up at half-past six. This will not be a blue jean and t-shirt affair. Dress nicely, pretend you're classy."

I let that last statement go. "Can I bring something?"

"Just yourself, and maybe don't schedule anything for tomorrow morning."

That sounded like an excellent plan to me, and I hung up.

Fifty-seven

Aaron called toward the end of the afternoon. "Just wanted to say thanks for coming down and giving your statement this morning. Sorry I wasn't there."

"So not a problem. God forbid you didn't have anything else to do. I have to say, Manning was almost civil. I wasn't sure he recognized me."

Aaron let that comment go and said, "Darcel Renard, the museum guy, identified Maynor Bouchard this morning, then waxed eloquent about the violence in America and our fetish for guns over the next half-hour. He's down examining the paintings as we speak."

"I'm not sure he's wrong about the violence and guns."

"French authorities sent images of the two Bouchards, Maynor and Pascal, along with a laundry list of suspected incidents dating back almost two decades. From what I could decipher, it looks like they were never charged with anything, let alone convicted."

"It's like something out of a movie. I don't suppose you've got any news on Demarcus?"

"The only news is no news. Not so much as a trace of him until last night. Ever since the Bouchards first broke into your place, it's like he just slipped beneath the

Art Hound ♦ 283

waves. More than a little strange, especially just leaving everything there, you'd think he would have made an effort to get it before they made off with the stuff. Then again, maybe he did, and you and Colleen Lacy escaping cut the plan short. I'm of the opinion something will turn up, a hotel room, an apartment, something, somewhere."

"You talk to Cherri or Darcy or whatever the hell name she's going by today?"

"Today, and for some time to come, she'll be going by her real name, Larue Desesperee."

"Hmmm, it's starting to make some sense why she changed it to Cherri."

"You curious what it means, her name?"

"Her name has a meaning?"

"Loosely translated, it means 'desperate woman of the street.'"

"What?"

"What can I say? Apparently, her parents had an inkling."

"Or they were nuts."

"Yeah, that too. She's in custody. We brought her over from the hospital this morning. She sounded cooperative in the initial interview, but she's all lawyered up now, so we'll see what develops. I'm guessing she'll try and cut a deal. I'm just not sure we're all that interested in dealing. Possible connection to two murders, definite connection to two kidnappings, not to mention last night, she's going away for a stretch. I'm guessing if she goes to court, the soonest she would be in front of someone would be a month from now, maybe two.

"I only had a couple of minutes with her before the medical staff waved me off. If she's to be believed, and at this stage, I'm believing her, she was grabbed from behind by someone wearing a mask and gloves. We're about ninety-nine percent sure it was Demarcus. She had no idea Maynor Bouchard was in the trunk of that car until you guys pulled her out."

Aaron didn't mention Farrell Finley, and I didn't bring him up. We hung up after another minute or two. Then I headed home to get ready for a night of passion with Heidi.

Fifty-eight

I showered, shaved, put on a new pair of black trousers, a black shirt, and a grey suit coat. The only tie I had was a blue tie with a Christmas tree that played "Rudolph the Red Nose Reindeer" when you squeezed it, so that was out. I picked up a bottle of wine, something French that was on sale at Solo Vino, and some flowers on the way over to Heidi's.

She answered the door in a sexy black velvet dress, strapless, low-cut, and short. Tonight her hair was dyed a rich auburn color, beautiful. Things were shaping up to be a very memorable evening.

"Oh, Dev, thank you for dressing up for a change. That's perfect," she said, running her eyes up and down my ensemble. "Oh, you shouldn't have," she said, looking at the flowers and the bottle of wine, then giggled like a schoolgirl.

We sat in the dining room, sipping wine from Waterford glasses while something delicious baked out in the kitchen. Heidi had a plate of hors d'oeuvres set out on the dining room table. Her best silver was out, resting on linen napkins, and I recognized the plates on the table as her grandmother's china. The lights were turned off, and the room was illuminated by about a dozen candles. Over in the living room, a nice fire was going in the fireplace, more candles were lit on the mantle, and she had Pandora dialed into soft music playing on her sound system. Things were going perfectly, and the last thing I felt like mentioning was the dreadful events of the previous evening.

I figured the moon must be full, and whether she knew it or not, she was in one of her hormonal induced romantic moods. I was just thinking I should have taken a nap and rested up before I came over.

She took a long sip of wine and said, "Well, I suppose you're wondering what this is all about."

I smiled an understanding smile, shook my head, and said, "No, I'm not wondering. I actually happen to know what it's all about, it's one of the things I like about you, Heidi and just for the record, I think it's wonderful. It's one of the many things that makes you so special."

"What?"

"Come on, we both know what's going on. I know, in fact, I've known for quite some time. No offense, but it's my business to catch on to subtleties, and just for the record, you'll never, ever hear a complaint from me. I absolutely love it."

She took a larger sip. "Are you kidding me? He told you?"

Now it was my turn. "What do you mean, *he* told me? Who the hell are you talking about?"

"Dev, you just said you knew. We had a deal. He made me promise I wouldn't say a word. God, this totally ruins my surprise," she said and took two hearty gulps of wine.

"What in God's name are you talking about?"

"Demarcus, dopey. He told you?"

"What the hell do you mean, Demarcus?"

"Hey, no need to yell. He did this," she said. She suddenly reached down below the table and pulled out a thin package, wrapped in brown paper, maybe two by two-and-a-half-feet.

"Is that a Demarcus painting?" I said.

"Oh, so you didn't know. Good. He was worried you might find out where he was, and he made me promise to wait until today before I told you."

"Demarcus?"

"Yes, silly. Who did you think I meant? Where do you think he's been hiding for the past four days while you had your ceiling repaired? Remember? He told you he couldn't deal with all the plaster dust. Didn't he? God, you should see the look on your face. So much for catching on to subtleties, you goofball. So go ahead, open it up."

I wasn't sure what I did, but I must have given her a look.

"Oh, don't look so surprised. Go ahead. I think you're going to like it."

I carefully removed the brown paper, and there, staring back at me was the Auguste Renoir painting, Young Girl Bathing.

"Auguste Renoir, Young Girl Bathing, 1892," I said and just stared.

"Oh. My. God. *You* actually know about Pierre Auguste Renoir and the original painting. I had no idea." She couldn't hide the surprise in her voice, but then again, I was too shocked to answer. The painting was basically the same as the other Demarcus forgeries except that it was definitely Heidi's figure, including a mole on the side of her left breast. Heidi's figure was a little bit leaner and much better endowed than the original. The hair was the same color as Heidi's dye job tonight, but much longer, extending down to the middle of her back, and it was definitely Heidi's face.

"When in the hell did he do this?"

She half-laughed and said, "Where did you think he's been for the last few days?"

"He was here?"

"Oh, relax. Nothing really happened," she said, although when she said it, she looked away. She quickly followed up with, "So, what do you think?"

"I think we should call the police."

She laughed for a few seconds until I pulled out my cell and called Aaron.

"You're kidding? You're, you're really calling them?"

"Heidi, Demarcus was some international art forger. He's suspected in two murders, possibly a couple of kidnappings, there's a museum guy from Paris over here who . . . Hello, Aaron, Dev. You're not going to believe it, but I found out where Demarcus has been for the last few days. No, I'm there now."

Fifty-nine

It was after ten. Heidi was on her second bottle of wine. The dinner she'd made was out of the oven, cooled and sitting on the stove, untouched. Aaron had gone over the same questions with her a half-dozen times, and her story remained the same. Demarcus had contacted her the day they'd first met when he dropped into the house as I opened the front door. He'd probably gotten her number off my cellphone, then called, told her he found her attractive and wanted to paint her. He'd showed her one of his forgeries and said she'd be a much more appealing model. Heidi's house was where he'd landed when he disappeared, literally in plain sight the entire time.

Darcel Renard was with us in the dining room in his lab coat, white gloves, and magnifying glass attached to his eyeglasses, examining the painting of Heidi at the far end of the dining room table. "Nothing short of magnificent," he said and raised a glass of the wine I'd brought in a toast toward Heidi. "If Madame would be so kind as to allow, I should like to send documentation to you, on museum stationery, of course, attesting to the quality of this work, even though a forgery. I'm thinking, Lieutenant, of the possibility of a show, and certainly, this work might be the centerpiece."

"A show?" Aaron and Heidi said at the same time.

"Yes, a show of forgeries of Renoir's Young Girl Bathing. Your department has almost two dozen, plus this work, and what, of course, makes this particular piece unique is we would have photographs of the model herself. Oh, provided that would be acceptable to Madame?" he said, addressing Heidi.

"Me? The center of an art show in Paris?"

"Oui, but of course. Well, and then we would want you to attend. This sounds like an idea?"

"Yes, it sounds like a wonderful idea. I'll do it. I'd love it." She took a sip of wine, then set her glass down. "Do you want to take the pictures now?" she asked, then reached behind her back and began to loosen the zipper on her dress.

"No, no, not yet. I'm thinking perhaps a professional, using the same pose and lighting as the painting. You would arrange this. Of course, we, the Musée d'Orsay, would be only too happy to pay for the photography and your flight and accommodations. This is good, no."

"Yes, yes," she said.

"I'll contact you tomorrow, Miss Bauer. Thank you for your time," Aaron said. "Shall we go, Mr. Renard?"

Darcel placed a limp hand in mine for a nanosecond, then turned, took Heidi's hand, and kissed it. "I look forward to having you as my guest in Paris, Madame," he said and followed Aaron out the door.

Once they were gone, I turned to Heidi and said, "God, you can't make it up. I'll give him this much. He's got great taste in paintings." I nodded at the painting as Heidi took it and set it on top of her dining room buffet, then stepped back and looked at the painting for a long moment. "Here's to me," she said and raised her wine glass in a toast.

"Yeah, to you," I said, then popped the top on my beer can and took a long sip.

The End

If you enjoyed **Art Hound** please take a moment and write a review.

It really helps. Thank you.

Don't miss the following sample of **The Office.** The next work of genius in the Dev Haskell Private Investigator series.

Sneak Peek

The Office

Second Edition

MIKE FARICY

Prologue

I'd stopped in for just one at The Spot with my attorney and officemate, Louie Laufen. That was two hours ago.

"God, I can't believe it," Louie said. He was off his stool, patting down his trouser pockets and his wrinkled pinstriped suit coat. "I thought for sure I put my wallet in my pocket before we came over."

Mike, the bartender, shot me a look. We were both just as sure he purposely left it in his desk drawer. It seemed to be almost second nature.

"I suppose I could run over and grab it if I can find it," Louie said, giving me a look as he spoke.

"Relax, I'll get it. Go on. You better get out of here if you're going to make that meeting. You can catch me next time."

"You sure, man?"

Like I had an option. "Yeah, I'll get it, no sweat. Hey, Mike," I called. "As long as I'm buying, maybe just one more beer, then cut me off so I get home in one piece."

"See you tomorrow, dude, and thanks," Louie said. "Hey, I've got a court appearance first thing, so I won't be in until ten, maybe eleven if things go my way."

"Safe drive home," I said, grabbing the fresh beer Mike slid across the bar.

As Louie walked out the door, an attractive looking woman stepped in. She was dressed in white shorts that looked like they had been spray-painted on and a halter top that looked a size or two, too small. Her dark hair was pulled back in a ponytail.

"Dev Haskell?" she said, looking at Mike and me. We were the only two people in the bar. It was league play night for The Spot softball team, and the regulars wouldn't be here until sometime close to 9:00.

"Yeah, that's me," I said and took a sip. It looked like my luck was beginning to change.

"Hi, Mr. Haskell. A friend said I should find you, but well, it's kind of a personal matter. Could I maybe talk to you outside?"

"Mike won't listen in, and even if he did, he wouldn't remember," I said.

"It's, ahh, of a *very* personal nature. You might find it enjoyable," she said and sort of looked embarrassed as she fiddled with her thumbs and index fingers.

I was off the stool in a second and standing next to her at the door. She had bright blue eyes that seemed to sparkle, pearly white teeth and a gorgeous complexion. The rest of her wasn't all that bad either.

She looked me up and down then said, "Mmm-hmm, my friend wasn't lying. Come on outside, honey, and let's talk."

I quickly followed her outside. She walked over to a black Mercedes, an AMG G-63. The windows were tinted so dark I couldn't see inside. "Here this will give us some privacy," she said.

My immediate thought was things were really going my way until the rear window was suddenly lowered, and Tubby Gustafson stuck his red nose, the size of a baked potato, out the window. As he did so, the driver's door swung open, and Fat Freddy Zimmerman hurried around the front of the car, waving a twenty-dollar bill.

"Here you go, Cindy, thanks," he said and handed the twenty to the woman.

She shoved the bill into her halter top and said, "Not a problem, happy to help." She didn't take the time to give me as much as a second look and just walked away.

"Get in," Tubby said to me, then raised his window.

As Fat Freddy led me around to the driver's side, I said, "Hey, what's this about?"

"Come on, man. You should know better than to ask that, just get in," he said and opened the rear door.

I climbed into the backseat next to Tubby. Fat Freddy slid behind the wheel and put the car in gear.

"Hey, wait, guys, not so fast. I got a tab going in there and a fresh beer on the bar."

"Amazing. Not." Tubby said. "And by the way, you're already trying my patience here. Now, buckle up, Haskell, and please, don't touch anything."

"But . . ." The look from Tubby pretty much put a stop to any questions I may have felt like asking.

One

Fat Freddy pulled into a secluded scenic parking area overlooking the Mississippi River. The parking area was surrounded by a three-foot-high limestone wall and then a thick hedge, maybe another two feet higher directly behind the limestone wall. I knew from experience years back that the place was popular after dark with the high school crowd. Freddy parked at the far end, jumped out, and ran around the car to open Tubby's door.

"Pleasure me with your attention, Haskell," Tubby said, and slowly oozed out of the backseat.

I figured that meant I should join him, and I opened the door then walked around to the rear of the car. At the moment, we were the only vehicle in the parking area. A black SUV, I think a Cadillac Escalade, pulled across the entrance, effectively blocking anyone's attempt to enter. Not that anyone was going to try to drive in with the two muscle-bound thugs sitting in the front seat.

"Let's enjoy the view, Haskell," Tubby said and walked toward the bluff. A solid rock wall dropped straight down for maybe thirty feet with a handful of large boulders scattered around the bottom. As a sixteen-year-old, I'd had an unfortunate encounter with root beer flavored schnapps one night in this very spot. I'd never quite recovered, avoiding any and all contact with the stuff for two decades.

"Lovely view, isn't it?" Tubby said. From this distance, the river appeared to flow gently around the bend and then on through the downtown area. "Come over here, Haskell, don't tell me you're afraid of heights."

"No, sir, not at all. I just don't like to tempt fate."

Tubby nodded like this made sense. "Here's the thing, Haskell. Against my better judgment, I'm going to send some business your way. No, no, no. No need to thank me. It's the least I can do. In the past, you've never seemed to fail to disappoint, but foolish me, I'm going to give you yet another opportunity."

"What kind of business are we talking here?"

"A distant acquaintance of mine, a gentleman by the name of Ozzie Frick, will be contacting you tomorrow. Let me thank you in advance for helping him."

"What does he want?"

"That's one of the many reasons you remain so unsuccessful, Haskell. You ask too many questions. You just take care of him, and things will work out."

"But I don't even know what—"

"Haskell, take a look at this," Tubby said and stepped right up next to the edge of the cliff. There was a small rock close to the edge, Tubby kicked it up into the air, and we both focused on it as it sailed off the cliff, then arched downward and bounced off one of the boulders below. "It's such a long way down, and then there's all those boulders, not at all what I'd call comforting. Now, any questions? Good," he answered for me. "Maybe stay here and study the view until it begins to resonate somewhere in that thick skull of yours. I'll expect a full report once you meet with Ozzie. Thank you," he said, then proceeded to walk back to his car.

"Hey, Tub . . . err, ahh, Mr. Gustafson," I called. "Would it be all right if you maybe gave me a lift back to The Spot. See, I've got an important meeting later tonight out in Burnsville, and well, my car is still parked down at The Spot."

Fat Freddy opened the rear door, and Tubby climbed in. Once he had settled into the backseat, Freddy closed the door then smiled, and gave me a little wave.

"Freddy, you can't leave me here. It's like five miles back."

Freddy ignored me, hurried around to the driver's side, and climbed in. I heard the locks on the doors click a moment later, and they drove off with the Escalade following closely behind.

I stepped over to the edge of the cliff. Tubby had been right, it was a long way down. I had five miles to cover before I got back to The Spot, so I started walking.

Two

I woke up early the next morning. Sophie was still asleep. She lay on her side, facing me with her pillow pulled over her head, and the sheet tucked under her arm. I stared for a long moment examining the curve of her hip beneath the sheet, weighing the odds of trying to wake her. I decided it probably wasn't worth the risk. She could have a short fuse from time to time, and past experience had taught me that waking her in the early morning was never going to go my way. I quietly slipped out of bed, stepped into my boxers, and headed out to her living room. Her dog, Lilly, a chocolate lab, sort of half-opened one eye, then wiggled down a little further in her bed and went back to sleep.

Sophie lived in the suburb of Burnsville, on Alimagnet lake, about twenty miles outside of Saint Paul. It was a gorgeous area and a lovely lake. The opposite shore was all parkland and, at this hour of the day, completely quiet. I stared out at the lake through the living room window for a few moments. There was a light fog on the water with the sun just beginning to come over the treetops on the eastern shore. I put the coffee on, then tried to figure out which one of the three remotes turned on the tv. After about ten minutes of pushing different buttons, I gave up, poured myself a mug of coffee, and just sat there, staring out the window.

We'd met a few months back in school, Dog Obedience school. Sophie's dog, Lilly, got first in class, but then Sophie was the instructor. Morton, my Golden retriever, earned a five percent discount ticket should we want to enroll in the beginner's session again. I guess the good news was Sophie and I sort of hit it off. Friends with benefits. We seemed to get together every so often and enjoyed each other's company. We had an unspoken rule that whoever hosted last time was the guest the next time around.

I settled onto the couch and stared out at the lake, sipping coffee, and watching as the fog slowly dissipated. I was obsessing about my upcoming meeting with Tubby's friend Ozzie Frick. I didn't know anything about the man other than Tubby Gustafson basically promised to kill me if I didn't meet with him. Not exactly the best introduction. I figured whatever the guy wanted me to do, I would just tell him it was out of my league. Maybe say something like the Feds were taking an interest in whoever hired me, and it might be in his best interest to get as far away from me as quickly as possible.

I was on my third cup of coffee when I heard the bathroom door close. Sophie wandered into the living room, rubbing the sleep from her eyes a few minutes later. She was dressed in a silk dressing gown, burgundy with white trim. She'd tied her dark hair up in a bun on top of her head, and she was barefoot.

"You okay, Dev? How long have you been up?"

I glanced at the clock sitting on her fireplace mantel. It was just a little after seven.

"I guess a couple of hours. You want me to get you a coffee?"

"No, thanks, baby. I can get it. Anything bugging you? You seemed kind of preoccupied, once you finally got here last night."

"Oh, sorry. I told you about the client I met with last night. I'm not really all that fond of the guy, to begin with, he contacted me and wants me to meet with someone he knows. I don't want—"

"So, tell him no, or tell him you can't because you're too busy."

"Mmm-mmm, no, it's not really that kind of a deal."

"Oh, well, if he's a good customer and he's sending a lot of business your way, maybe you should just do it." She was at the kitchen counter now, filling her coffee mug. I was still staring out at the lake and heard the refrigerator door open. I waited for what I knew was coming.

"I thought I got two of these. What the—? Dev? Did you eat one of these caramel rolls?"

"I was starving, and they looked so good."

"We were going to share them and talk, remember? We agreed to have a conversation about our relationship this morning, where things are going. God."

"Well, this way, I won't be starving, and I'll be able to pay more attention to everything you say."

She gave me a long look, shook her head and muttered something, as she pulled a plate out of a kitchen cabinet and set it on the counter. She placed the caramel roll on the plate, then proceeded to cut it in half.

"Get your butt over here."

Thank God, she didn't say *'We need to talk'* because when a guy hears that, he automatically knows things just aren't going to go his way. I picked up my coffee mug and gave a last look out at the lake. The sun was up over the trees, and some sort of yellow bird, I think a goldfinch, was out on the deck flitting back and forth between two bird feeders. I gave the thing a longing look before I headed over to the kitchen counter, sat down on one of the wooden stools, took a deep breath, and braced myself.

Sophie pushed half of the caramel roll in front of me, topped up both our coffee mugs then took a sip. In the few short minutes she'd been in the living room, she had somehow loosened her silk dressing gown so it almost, but never quite revealed some of the attributes that kept me returning.

I took a sip of coffee, then reached for half of the caramel roll and said, "Okay, what's on your mind?"

"I really think we need to talk," she said.

Things went downhill from there.

Three

I somehow managed to escape Sophie's without being stabbed by a kitchen knife or getting doused with hot coffee. Just now, I was looking out my office window through binoculars, trying to catch sight of one of the women in the third-floor apartment across the street. I was beginning to think no one was home.

I watched as Louie pulled up across the street and waited for a car to park so he could back into the other open space. Louie was driving a blue Volkswagen Jetta. The thing was nothing if not boring. It was also nine years newer and a thousand times better than my 2003 Honda Accord. I already had the brakes replaced not once but twice, along with a new transmission last fall, but I digress.

I watched as Louie waited while the Mercedes backed into the parking spot then pulled ahead just enough to be perfectly positioned exactly in the middle of two parking spaces.

Louie apparently didn't honk, give the guy the finger or swear out the window like I would. Instead, he drove down to the far end of the block and grabbed a spot, not that the walk back wouldn't do him good.

I watched as a guy with a shaved head, mirrored sunglasses, and a grey strappy t-shirt climbed out of the Mercedes, pressed the lock button on his key fob, then hurried across the street and into our building. A moment later, I heard heavy footsteps coming up the stairs.

"You Haskell?" He said as he stood in the open doorway. He apparently didn't feel the need to take the sunglasses off. For some reason, I hadn't noticed it before, but there was a red cross on the front of his strappy t-shirt and below that the words *'Orgasm Donor'*. Morton got up and headed toward him, tail wagging. The guy shot a disapproving look in his direction, causing Morton to stop midway and hurry back to where he'd been sleeping in front of the file cabinet. He curled up on his pillow and sort of hid his face.

"You must be Ozzie Frick," I said, sounding more like an accusation than a question.

"Tubby filled you in?"

"No, not really, more like he said you had a problem, and you'd like me to take a look at it, but he didn't give me any specifics."

He sort of nodded and sat down in front of my desk. He pushed the stack of files at the edge of my desk toward the center, then tipped the client chair back and placed two cowboy boots on top of my desk. I'd been right all along. I wasn't going to like this guy.

"So, tell me about your problem."

"Nosey neighbor," he said.

"What?"

"Someone poking around into my private business."

"You talk to them?"

He half scoffed and shook his head. "We had words, didn't seem to do much good. I need her to back the hell off."

"What exactly is she doing?"

"Writing down the license numbers of my . . . customers. Anyone who stops in for a moment. She has a bullhorn, and she shouts their damn license number out, calls them all sorts of names, and then tells them she's calling the police."

"And are they doing anything illegal, or maybe the better question is, are you?"

He lowered his head and looked at me over the top of his mirrored sunglasses. "What I'm doing ain't the point here."

"It might be if she's calling the police. What did they say? Have you talked to them?"

"The cops? You gotta be kidding me. Did you listen to what I just said? She's taking down their license numbers and—"

"Yeah, I heard that part. Right off the top, it sounds like you're selling drugs or God knows what and no offense, but you gotta be nuts to think I'd help you with that sort of enterprise."

"But Tubby said you'd help."

I couldn't figure out if this Ozzie was really that stupid or if Tubby was setting me up. I thought about it for a half-second then said, "Tell you what, let me check into this. Where's this woman with the bullhorn live?"

He pulled an envelope from his pocket, unfolded it, and tossed the thing in my general direction. An address was scribbled across the back. "Here's her address. Her name is Debbie or Doris or something like that, don't know her last name. A real bitch. I tried to be nice once, but she wasn't having none of it. You're my last shot at being a good guy. You don't work out, all bets are off."

I could only imagine. Something wasn't right, and my first thought was *this woman was probably in more danger than she realized.* "I'll check her out this afternoon. For the time being, stay away from her. Let me check and see what, if anything, she's reported to the police."

"You'll keep me posted?" he said, slowly pulling his cowboy boots off my desk then groaning as he stood up.

I heard the building door close downstairs on the first floor, and then a familiar wheeze as Louie slowly made his way up the stairs.

"I need to have this dealt with right quick. Tubby said, you're the man."

"I'll see what I can do," I said, just as red-faced Louie stumbled into the office.

"Appreciate it. By the way, Tubby said this would be a freebie, said you owed him, big time."

Louie's eyes grew wide when Ozzie turned, gave him a nod, and headed out the door. Ozzie was out of the building and waiting for a bus to pass so he could cross the street before Louie was able to talk.

"That, that's the bastard that took up two parking places. I had to park about a mile away. I wasn't sure I was gonna be able to make it back to the office."

"Yeah, I know I was watching it out the window," I said and picked up the binoculars. I focused on Ozzie's license plate. It was from Illinois, and I wrote down the number. "If you hurry, you can see him getting back into that Mercedes. That space is going to be open. You could get back in your car and grab it."

Louie flopped into the chair behind the picnic table he used as a desk and loosened his tie. "If I never saw that parking hog again, it would be too soon. What was he doing up here?"

"Tubby Gustafson sent him."

"Tubby? Since when has anything he's been involved with ever worked out well for you?"

"Believe me, don't I know, and Tubby told him I'd help for free. God. That jerk. His name's Ozzie Frick, has a beef with a neighbor who's taking down license numbers and yelling over a bull horn at the people that are coming to see him."

"What?"

"Yeah. She sounds like an irate neighbor who's probably not too happy with that jackass selling drugs near her home."

"Figures he'd be involved in something like that. Gee, imagine. What do they hope to get from you?"

"That's the part that isn't making any sense. I'm going to go see her and if nothing else warn her and suggest she might want to be in touch with the police if she hasn't been already. It sounds like the screwiest damn thing. I can't quite figure out what Tubby's angle is in this."

Four

The address was over on the east side of town. An area that had experienced more than it's fair share of problems over the past fifty years. Like so many sections of town, there was a steady decline as manufacturing pulled out, housing prices fell. What had once been a strong working-class area was gradually carved up and whittled away. Shops along the main arteries began to close, single-family homes were broken up into multiple units, and opportunity seemed to disappear.

The address Ozzie had given me was on a dead-end street, six doors from a railroad line that, for all practical purposes, was now dormant. The factories the area had once served had already been gone for more than a quarter of a century.

The homes along the street were probably a century old, built just before or after the First World War. I guessed at least half of them were multiple units, everything from a duplex to five or six small efficiencies based on the mailboxes attached to the front of the houses. The address I'd been given appeared to still be a single-family home. The grass was cut, and a hedge along the front porch appeared neatly trimmed. The house looked freshly painted. The lapped wood siding was green with cream-colored trim and sort of a dark red accent color. The double front doors were painted black, and each had a panel of beveled glass. Three wooden steps led up to the front porch. A porch swing hung on the far end of the porch, and a woman who looked to be maybe sixtyish was sitting on the swing. I pulled over and parked.

My Honda Accord sort of groaned and sputtered for about ten seconds before shutting down completely. As I climbed out, I was aware she was watching me. I smiled and nodded as I stepped onto the sidewalk, but the moment I began to head onto her property, a vicious, deep-throated growl erupted from the porch, and some sort of wild-eyed animal was suddenly straining at a chain in an effort to get to me.

"I'd say you've gone just about far enough. What do you want?"

"I'm looking for Debbie or Doris, not sure which it is."

"It's Daisy, and this is my house, so what do you want?"

"I'd like to talk to you if I could," I had to raise my voice to be heard over the continuous barking and growling.

"I ain't the least bit interested in whatever it is you're selling if that's what this is all about."

"No ma'am, nothing like that. I, umm, understand you might be dealing with a problem at the end of your block." I nodded toward the dead end.

She seemed to eye me cautiously for a moment then said, "Axel, enough," and the dog immediately stopped barking. "Who told you that?"

"Neighborhood gossip. I just wanted to warn you. I don't think you're dealing with some very nice people."

"You threatening me?" Suddenly there was an edge to her voice. Axel, the dog, raised his head and seemed to take a renewed interest in me.

"No ma'am, I would just suggest that you be careful, maybe contact the police if you haven't yet. If you're taking down makes of cars, license numbers, and maybe the times those cars are here, you should give the cops that information. Sometimes it takes a while, but if you can establish a pattern, it can help them in shutting things down."

"What's your name?"

"Haskell, Dev Haskell. Actually, I'm a private investigator, so I deal with the police a good bit of the time."

"Maybe you'd like to come up on the porch, so we're not having to yell back and forth."

"Is your dog going to be okay with that?"

"Axel? He'll get used to you, just don't move too fast and you should be okay. His bark is worse than his bite."

Not exactly encouraging. I took two or three tentative steps toward the porch and heard the links on Axel's chain suddenly drag across the wooden porch floor. He waited at the top step, eyes flared, and teeth showing. He growled and dared me to step onto the front porch.

"That's just his way of saying hello," she said. "Now Axel, you be nice, don't bite. You know I don't like that."

Axel took a step toward me, bared his teeth again and barked some more.

"Maybe if I just stayed down here, we could talk."

"Don't be silly. He just wants to let you know he's doing his job."

"Yeah, not to worry, I got that message loud and clear."

"Axel, get back here," she said and yanked on the heavy chain connected to his choke collar. "Come on, come on, Axel, you get back here."

He seemed to grudgingly give way, as I cautiously climbed up the front steps.

"Come on up, Mr. Hassle. I'd say he likes you."

"Oh great, I'd hate to see him when he didn't."

Axel was at her feet now, watching my every move, teeth bared and still growling. At least he wasn't barking and lurching toward me.

"Please, take a seat," she said, pointing to a pressed-back wooden chair that looked like it might have been original to the house.

I could feel the sweat in my armpits and a long drop running down my back. I smiled at Axel, being sure not to show any teeth.

His growl turned deeper, no doubt he sensed my fear.

"I think he likes you."

"I'd hate to see him mad," I said and tried to ignore the growls.

To be continued . . .

Gee, imagine, Sophie forgot to 'catch' Dev in the morning. That's not the only thing that isn't going to go Dev's way. Better grab your copy of **The Office**, and see if things eventually work out for him…

Books by Mike Faricy
Crime Fiction Firsts

A boxset of the first four books in four crime fiction series:

    Russian Roulette; Dev Haskell series
    Welcome; Jack Dillon Dublin Tales series
    Corridor Man; Corridor Man series
    Reduced Ransom! Hot Shot series

The following titles comprise the Dev Haskell series:

    Russian Roulette: Case 1
    Mr. Swirlee: Case 2
    Bite Me: Case 3
    Bombshell: Case 4
    Tutti Frutti: Case 5
    Last Shot: Case 6
    Ting-A-Ling: Case 7
    Crickett: Case 8
    Bulldog: Case 9
    Double Trouble: Case 10
    Yellow Ribbon: Case 11
    Dog Gone: Case 12
    Scam Man: Case 13
    Foiled: Case 14
    What Happens in Vegas… Case 15
    Art Hound: Case 16
    The Office: Case 17

Star Struck: Case 18
International Incident: Case 19
Guest From Hell: Case 20
Art Attack: Case 21
Mystery Man: Case 22
Bow-Wow Rescue: Case 23
Cold Case: Case 24
Cash Up Front: Case 25
Dream House: Case 26
Alley Katz: Case 27
The Big Gamble: Case 28
Bad to the Bone: Case 29
Silencio!: Case 30
Surprise, Surprise: Case 31
Hit & Run: Case 32
Suspect Santa: Case 33
P.I. Apprentice: Case 34
Rebel Without a Clue: Case 35

The following titles are Dev Haskell novellas:
Dollhouse
The Dance
Pixie
Fore!
Twinkle Toes
(*a Dev Haskell short story*)

The following are Dev Haskell Boxsets:
Dev Haskell Boxset 1-3
Dev Haskell Boxset 4-6
Dev Haskell Boxset 7-9
Dev Haskell Boxset 10-12
Dev Haskell Boxset 13-15
Dev Haskell Boxset 16-18
Dev Haskell Boxset 19-21
Dev Haskell Boxset 22-24
Dev Haskell Boxset 25-27
Dev Haskell Boxset 28-30
Dev Haskell Boxset 1-7
Dev Haskell Boxset 8-14
Dev Haskell Boxset 15-19
Dev Haskell Boxset 20-24
Dev Haskell Boxset 25-29

The following titles comprise the Jack Dillon Dublin Tales series:
Welcome
Jack Dillon Dublin Tale 1
Sweet Dreams
Jack Dillon Dublin Tale 2
Mirror Mirror
Jack Dillon Dublin Tale 3
Silver Bullet
Jack Dillon Dublin Tale 4
Fair City Blues
Jack Dillon Dublin Tale 5

Spade Work
Jack Dillon Dublin Tale 6
Madeline Missing
Jack Dillon Dublin Tale 7
Mistaken Identity
Jack Dillon Dublin Tale 8
Picture Perfect
Jack Dillon Dublin Tale 9
Dublin Moon
Jack Dillon Dublin Tale 10
Mystery Woman
Jack Dillon Dublin Tale 11
Second Chance
Jack Dillon Dublin Tale 12
Payback Brother
Jack Dillon Dublin Tale 13
The Heist
Jack Dillon Dublin Tale 14
Jewels To Kill For
Jack Dillon Dublin Tale 15
Retirement Scheme
Jack Dillon Dublin Tale 16
The Collector
Jack Dillon Dublin Tale 17

Jack Dillon Dublin Tales Boxsets:
Jack Dillon Dublin Tales 1-3
Jack Dillon Dublin Tales 4-6
Jack Dillon Dublin Tales 1-5

Jack Dillon Dublin Tales 1-7
Jack Dillon Dublin Tales 6-10

The following titles comprise the Hotshot series;
Reduced Ransom! Second Edition
Finders Keepers! Second Edition
Bankers Hours Second Edition
Chow Down Second Edition
Moonlight Dance Academy Second Edition
Irish Dukes (Fight Card Series)
written under the pseudonym Jack Tunney

The following titles comprise the Corridor Man series:
Corridor Man
Corridor Man 2: Opportunity knocks
Corridor Man 3: The Dungeon
Corridor Man 4: Dead End
Corridor Man 5: Finger
Corridor Man 6: Exit Strategy
Corridor Man 7: Trunk Music
Corridor Man 8: Birthday Boy
Corridor Man 9: Boss Man
Corridor Man 10: Bye Bye Bobby

Corridor Man novellas:
Corridor Man: Valentine
Corridor Man: Auditor
Corridor Man: Howling

Corridor Man: Spa Day

The following are Corridor Man Boxsets:
Corridor Man Boxset 1-3
Corridor Man Boxset 1-5
Corridor Man Boxset 6-9

All books are available on Amazon.com

Thank you!

Contact the author:
- Email: mikefaricyauthor@gmail.com
- Twitter: @Mikefaricybooks
- Facebook: Mike Faricy Author
- Website: http://www.mikefaricybooks.com

Published by

MJF Publishing